Idea

by Ja... ~~by Jared Holiday, age 36~~

I. Physical Beauty
- Petite frame, but negotiable as long as it looks good
- Takes great care of her person; always looks perfect day and night

II. Social Abilities
- Understands the importance of entertaining for her husband's (my) career

III. Personal Likes and Dislikes *Oh, for goodness sake!*
- Defers to husband's opinions, career and needs above her own
- Calm nature; prefers smoothing matters over to fighting

IV. Most Important *What was I thinking?*
- Cooks like a pro
- Is a tigress in bed
- Love is not a requisite for her for marriage

25% JH, age 36
~~75%~~

NOTE: Candidates must reach ~~90%~~ of attributes for serious consideration.

Dear Reader,

You're about to meet the third Holiday cousin, Jared, who joins Peter, Michael and Raymond. They're four sexy guys with two things in common: the Holiday name and humbug in the heart! But this year, Cupid's working overtime and by Christmas he's aiming to have the Holiday men singing love songs!

From the creative mind of Linda Cajio comes THE HOLIDAY HEART miniseries. Here, Jared learns that all work and no play makes for a dull Labor Day. Linda's already taken us through Valentine's Day and Mother's Day; don't miss the last Holiday cousin's story at Christmas.

Linda Cajio is a name well-known to readers of romance fiction. She's the author of over twenty bestselling contemporary and historical romances, a past president of Romance Writers of America and the winner of many writing awards. Linda makes her home in New Jersey, with her family.

Be sure you don't miss any of the Holiday men in THE HOLIDAY HEART series!

Regards,

Debra Matteucci
Senior Editor & Editorial Coordinator
Harlequin Books
300 East 42nd Street
New York, NY 10017

BOSS MAN
Linda Cajio

Harlequin Books

TORONTO • NEW YORK • LONDON
AMSTERDAM • PARIS • SYDNEY • HAMBURG
STOCKHOLM • ATHENS • TOKYO • MILAN
MADRID • WARSAW • BUDAPEST • AUCKLAND

ISBN 0-373-16694-X

BOSS MAN

Printed in U.S.A.

Prologue

IDEAL-MATE ATTRIBUTES
by Jared Holiday
I. Physical Beauty

    A. Dark hair, straight; preferably sophisticated style

    B. Doelike brown eyes

    C. Exotic features, delicate

    D. Creamy skin, absolutely unblemished

    E. Large breasts

    F. Small waist

    G. Long, slender legs

    H. Petite frame, but negotiable as long as it looks good

    I. Two years younger than husband (me)

II. Intelligence

    A. MBA, at least

    B. Attended Ivy League school

    C. Have had at least one scholarship for grade-point average

    D. Shrewd in personal finances
    E. Can assess people and situations quickly

III. Personal Background

   A. Personal wealth preferable, enough to live comfortably
   B. Parents, relatives have personal wealth/no bums
   C. Family name of some social standing
   D. Race unimportant, but prefer Asian

IV. Career

   A. Well along her corporate ladder
   B. Has a commitment to her job
   C. Totally understands husband's needs with his job
   D. Does not plan to interrupt career for family

V. Social Abilities

   A. Adapts to any situation
   B. Can talk with anybody about anything, knowledgeably
   C. Thrives on social situations
   D. Loves to entertain; last-minute guests are never a problem
   E. Understands the importance of entertaining for husband's career
   F. Will further her husband's cause in any way she can
   G. Is active in at least two community organizations

VI. Personal Likes and Dislikes

A. Takes great care of her person; always looks perfect day and night
B. Is a tigress in bed
C. Defers to husband's opinions, career and needs above her own
D. Wants two children and will be a very giving mother to them
E. Likes nouvelle cuisine—cooks like a pro
F. Likes plays
G. Likes symphonies
H. Likes foreign films over domestic
I. Dresses in designer clothes, European flair
J. Likes jazz over other types of music
K. Generally very upscale in her total outlook
L. Calm nature; prefers smoothing matters over to fighting

VII. Most Important

A. Love is not a requisite for her for marriage
B. She sees the value of good companionship and sharing similar interests with her husband
C. Although not a proponent of open marriage for herself, she will turn the occasional blind eye to her husband's outside needs

NOTE: Candidates must reach 90% of attributes for serious consideration.

Jared Holiday put the last note on the paper with a flourish. He read over his list, proud that he had figured out at age twenty what he wanted in a woman. Some of the ideals were high, maybe even impossible to achieve in a woman, but one had to aim high. Lowering a standard was a mistake many people made. It might take awhile to find his ideal wife, but he was willing to wait. Besides, he still had college, then law school to finish and his own career to establish.

He'd seen what love could do, and it wasn't good. People didn't think things out when they fell in love. And "love" at first sight was all gonads and obsession. Hardly love. He refused to be that foolish. Knowing what one wanted ensured he'd avoid the trap of love. He'd have the ideal woman instead. That was far more important.

Jared looked at the little statute of Justice on his desk. She kept her eyes covered and her scales balanced. She looked damn good, too.

He smiled wistfully. Now, if only he could find a girl like her...

Chapter One

Jared Holiday took one look and fell in love.

The object of his spontaneous emotion glided through the glass doors of the law offices of Davis, Hansen and Davis, Wynnewood, Pennsylvania. Her feet didn't touch the ground once. Well, they might have, he later would concede, but he never was quite sure.

E.J. had arranged for his Labor Day rescue in the form of a temporary secretary. This couldn't be her, he thought. This was an angel. E.J. *never* got angels from the temp agency.

Her body was slight, almost skinny, yet she moved sinuously, every graceful sway of her hips tearing another delicious rip in his body. His heart pounded. No air reached his lungs, no matter how hard he tried to breathe. His blood pumped frantically in his veins. His ears rang. Never had he known pain could feel so good. Her plaid, summer jumper reached her calves, yet left her arms bare. Silver dangled at her wrists and throat, and her slender feet were wrapped in delicate sandals. Pink nail polish highlighted each toe. He couldn't be getting a foot fetish, he thought, but the notion tempted.

She carried an oversize tote bag. Even that somehow matched her.

Her strawberry blond hair hung free in thick waves past her shoulder blades. Her sky blue eyes gazed earnestly at him and he noted that freckles dusted her unpowdered features. Her face reminded him of Botticelli's *Venus* rising from the ocean—innocent, serene, seductive. Her mouth hinted at a knowing smile, as if she was well aware of her powerful effect on him. Somewhere his brain registered that he had seen far more beautiful women, but he couldn't remember any of them.

"Will you marry me?"

Jared wondered where the hoarse voice originated from, then realized it came from him. Him! A divorce lawyer. He couldn't have fallen in love at first sight, he thought. That was nonsense for books and songs. He didn't believe the phenomenon existed.

What the hell was he thinking?

The woman paused. "I beg your pardon?"

Her low voice, like aged, smooth whiskey over ice, sent shivers up his spine.

OK, so he was acting like an idiot. That didn't mean he was in love. Just stupid. The spell she wove lessened. Barely, but enough for him to function. What was he doing, anyway? Turning into his cousins, Peter and Michael? Peter had married at the beginning of the summer after a quick courtship. And Michael got snagged by a widow with six kids just a week ago. Maybe all this familial marrying was affecting him. Maybe he'd better get his head examined.

He cleared his throat. "I'm Jared Holiday."

"Alison Palmer from Tempmates," she said, extending her hand.

Jared stared at her long fingers, almost afraid to take

them in his own, afraid her touch would pack as much of a wallop as the rest of her did. *Get a grip, man,* he told himself. Literally. He reached out and firmly grasped her hand.

Lightning erupted before his eyes. Thunder boomed in his ears. Warm silk. Cool chocolate. Clinging satin. Descriptions rolled through his head one after another.

"Thanks for coming on Labor Day," he managed to say. "We really need the help, especially with the cases that need to be filed in court tomorrow morning."

"As long as you're paying me, that's OK."

She took her hand back and glanced away. He wondered if she felt the jolt he had. He hoped so and he hoped not. If she did, then he was glad he wasn't imagining the reaction. If she didn't, that meant he'd gone nuts, the best explanation he had for what was happening to him.

She glanced back. Her gaze seemed to focus on his shirt and tie. His body turned hot underneath his clothes.

She tucked a few stray strands of her marvelous hair behind her ear. His list of ideal attributes in a woman had brunettes as the best, but her strawberry blond hair fascinated him. God, there was so much of it.

"The agency said I could wear casual clothes for today." She touched her dress. "I hope they got it right. Sometimes agencies don't."

"No, it's fine," he said, realizing his obsessive need to always dress for the office had disconcerted her. "You look just fine. Great, in fact. That dress really becomes you...." He was babbling. Badly. "It's a holiday, so the office is technically closed. But I've got all this work that needs typing. I understand you have legal-secretary experience."

She nodded. "Just lead the way to a computer."

As he did, he admitted she didn't appear to be a legal secretary. At least not the ones Davis, Hansen and Davis had. They were all stodgy middle-aged women, with the exception of E.J., the office manager, who looked like a kid and acted like a drill sergeant. Alison looked like something out of Woodstock.

"My secretary quit on Friday morning," he explained, settling Alison in front of a desk strewn with papers. "She called in to announce she was getting married this weekend to a man she'd just met and that she wouldn't be back."

"Wow," Alison said, whistling. "I hope he's rich or good-looking, because that's the only way I'd elope like that."

Jared wondered how good-looking or rich a man had to be for her to drop everything and marry. Not nearly enough for himself, he bet.

Now why would he even think that way? Until a few minutes ago, he hadn't given marriage more than a passing glance. Jared had no answer. But Alison Palmer had walked through the doors, and his common sense had gone out the window.

He gathered it back in and got down to business, a state with which he was more than comfortable. Leaning over Alison's right shoulder, he whisked the mouse around, opening files on the monitor screen.

"These are my notes from my clients' meetings. You'll need the ones starred. You take them and fill in the brief forms from these files here."

He opened another computer file, but her perfume, a mix of flowers and sea scents, distracted him. All of her this close distracted him. He paused, savoring the faint freckles dotting her bare shoulders and chest. He'd never been a freckle man before, but he was now. They fascinated him, too, urging him to count each one, to follow each one to the next and see how much of her body was covered with the delicate blemishes.

The first swells of her breasts were just visible above the bodice of her jumper. The dress was modest enough but still provided a peek at heaven. A delicate necklace of silver and agate stones hung around her neck, a neck he wanted badly to kiss. Would her skin taste as sweet as it looked...?

"I assume you want me to put the notes with the briefs," Alison said pragmatically, pushing her chair slightly away from him.

Jared blinked, reality returning. "Oh. Yes, that's right. Basically you just have to merge them and fill in the language. Avoid using anything starred. That's information only I need to know for the case. Since you've done this sort of thing before, it shouldn't be too hard. Everything's on Wordway. You know how to use that program?"

"No problem." She looked at the monitor screen and the desk. She reached into her large tote bag and took out a coffeepot. "Mind if I plug this in?"

He straightened. "I've made coffee in the kitchen—"

"Oh, that's OK. I don't drink coffee. I use a special tea that needs scalding water, so I just bring my own pot to heat it in. Most commercial makers aren't really hot enough." She stood, her little pot in hand. "I'll just get some water. Since no one's here but us..."

It sounded so erotic from her lips.

"...Do you mind if I play my radio? I work better with background noise."

"Ah...no," he replied, nonplussed, wondering what else she had in that tote bag.

"Thanks." She smiled like the angel she was, making him feel as if everything would be all right.

"I'll show you to the kitchen," he added, trying to be cool and calm.

"Just point me in the right direction, and I'll find it," she replied. "You probably have work to do, especially if you have to work on Labor Day like this."

He loved to work, the holidays not a deterrent to him. He debated whether to debate with her, then decided against it. Besides, if he continued to stand this close to her for much longer, he wouldn't be responsible for his actions. "Down the hall, third door on your left."

"Thanks." She swished away, leaving him in a swirling scent of perfume and woman.

As soon as she disappeared into the kitchen, Jared ran for his office. Panting, he shut the door behind him and leaned against it, grateful to be in his refuge. He refused to lie to himself. Staying out there with Alison Palmer was dangerous. Damned dangerous.

What the hell was wrong with him? What was that stuff about marriage? He couldn't believe it had come from his mouth.

Her mouth, on the other hand, could drive him crazy....

A radio suddenly blared pop music—not loud enough to complain about, but loud enough for him to hear. He would have pegged her for a seventies retro-hard-rock fan. She looked like a flower child with her long hair, almost no makeup and flowing dress.

E.J. would be in later today. The firm's no-nonsense office manager would put a damper on his fantasies. E.J. could dampen a college frat party in full swing. She would have the *cajónes* to lecture God on his performance thus far with the universe.

Jared stared at the small statue of Justice sitting on his desktop. The feminine figure held the balanced scales with one hand and gripped the sword with her other. The blindfold, always a symbol of objectivity, covered her eyes. She was his ideal woman. Years ago, on a whim, he'd made a list of characteristics for his ideal mate based on some of the statue's attributes. When he found a woman who measured up to Justice he'd seriously consider marriage.

Whatever had happened to him out there was simply a sign of stress. That was it. His caseload was on overdrive; every woman in the Philadelphia area seeming to need a divorce. His secretary had quit for nonsense at the worst time, leaving him under even more stress. It had manifested itself in an odd way. Like steam from a teakettle, it had found an avenue of escape.

"OK," he said to the statue. "I'll see my doctor first thing in the morning."

Just to get the lid back on real tight.

ADULT DAY CAMP...against will...must please...have anguish, will travel...det....suf....hum...

Alison paused in her typing, baffled by the cryptic wording in Jared Holiday's notes. The radio played "La Macarina," its fast beat urging her to skip the nonsense notations and continue typing. Only she knew she couldn't. Not until she understood the Greek here.

But that meant close proximity to Jared Holiday.

She rubbed the fingers of her right hand, the hand that had touched his. They still tingled like electricity had shot through them. What had happened? From the moment she had walked in the door and looked at Jared, she'd had no answer. Only her heart had beat wildly in her chest. Her vision had faded. Her skin had tingled and her ears buzzed. Even the thought of approaching him had the sensations starting all over again.

Worse, she'd thought she'd heard him ask her to marry him. That was impossible. She must have been dreaming. She hoped so, since she'd had a momentary, yet tremendous urge to say yes.

Definitely dreaming.

She took a sip of her herb tea to right her equilibrium. Usually the tea soothed her, but not this time. She reminded herself she had a job to do, one in which she took great pride. She knew she didn't look like an FBI operative, but that was a blessing she played up because it allowed her more freedom to do her real job. The temp job was important, too, for personal satisfaction, so she'd better find out what Holiday was saying about Maryanne O'Malley and her soon-to-be ex-husband.

Alison turned the radio down and went to his office. Forcing herself to have no reaction to him, she knocked on the door. The moment he opened it, her heart raced, her blood flowed thickly in her veins and her breath came in pants. So much for no reaction.

He wasn't Brad Pitt, Tom Cruise, Keanu Reeves or any combination thereof. Why did she act as though he was? His features were sharply defined, almost craggy, yet his eyes were a soft blue. They make him look sensitive, vulnerable. He brushed his dark hair back from his forehead, the expensive cut ensuring not a hair went out of place when he did. The white silk shirt and paisley tie suited his broad shoulders and narrow waist. He didn't have the muscles or weight of a football player, but he looked good. Damn good.

She wondered if he thought she looked dowdy. Her hotel had missed her wake-up call, so she'd gotten up late and had grabbed the jumper and sandals, knowing she could dress casually. She'd skipped makeup except for mascara on her blond eyelashes. Now she wished she'd worn her best suit and heels. Anything that screamed sophistication, intelligence and glamour, like the ritzy law firm here on the Main Line. Like Jared...

God help her, Alison thought, staring at the law god at the desk before her. She was in deep trouble. This temp job was only a week long. It appeared it would be a *long* week where Jared Holiday was concerned.

"Yes?" he said finally.

"Oh." She shuddered, trying to shake out of her star-struck paralysis. "Hi. I can't decipher your notes. It's a nifty shorthand you're using, but a little too obscure for me."

"I'm sorry." Grinning, he came out of his office. "I forgot you wouldn't know the code."

"That's OK."

He went by her, leaving a trail of cologne and man. The combined scents had her head spinning. Damn, but he smelled good.

She followed him to the desk, where he stared at the computer screen. She stopped a safe distance away. He finally straightened. "Oh, boy. I forgot this one was in the mix."

She raised her eyebrows. "Is there a problem?"

He coughed and looked sheepish. "This is confidential. You understand that."

She bristled inwardly at his suggestion that she might not be circumspect. Logic told her, however, that he was only acting sensibly since he didn't know her. "Sure. Tempmates guarantees confidentiality. That's why they hire people who forget their name the moment after they say it. I understand. Honest."

This time he raised his eyebrows. And cute eyebrows

they were, too, with their slight arch. "Her husband attended an adult camp that specialized in...well, sex."

Alison could feel the flush creeping up her cheeks. The last thing she wanted to hear was that word from his lips. It was just too damned suggestive.

"...The client didn't know until she got there, although she stayed and participated to please him. He fell in love with someone he met at the camp and had an affair, committing adultery."

What, Alison wondered, would one call the camp "activities"? Arts and crafts in the nude? People amazed her. She could easily imagine Jared in the nude, stringing leather pouches. She tried not to. Maybe she ought to visit an adult camp. Clearly, she needed help in the "games" department like nobody's business.

"It left her with mental anguish, suffering and humiliation," Jared finished, gazing at Alison with those big, blue eyes.

"I see," she said, wishing she hadn't. Boy, what a conversation to have with a man she was attracted to and didn't want to be. The FBI policies-and-procedures manual didn't cover this. It didn't help her blush, either. "So that's the 'suf,' 'hum,' and 'have anguish.' But what's the 'will travel?'"

"The anguish came after the fact," he replied.

"Okey-dokey."

He must have some law practice, she thought. She didn't want to know, that was for sure. She reached over and pulled out the hard copies of the brief she had finished. "Here. You better check these."

"You did all this already?" he asked, taking the pages from her.

"Sure. Let's see if I've gotten it right, though. That's the trick." She sat back down in the chair. Looking at the monitor screen, she swallowed and said, "So you want me to say she went to sex camp and basically didn't like it. My mom would roll over in her grave if she knew I was writing this."

Sorry, Mom, she thought, sending a mental apology to her very alive mother in upstate New York.

He chuckled. "It could be worse, but that's the divorce business. Sometimes you wind up having to use the intimate details of a client's married life on her behalf."

"I could make a comment, but I won't. I might remember it." The radio began a lively rap song. For a moment, Alison rocked in her seat to get the rhythm, then began to type in time to the music.

Unfortunately, she was aware of Jared standing almost off her shoulder, reading, and faltered slightly in her work. What the heck was wrong with her? In her job, both real and cover, she had traveled widely and met many people, a facet she liked a great deal. She even met the occasional man who attracted her. She always controlled that reaction. Until now.

"These are terrific," he said, setting them back on the desk. "Clearly, you know what you're doing with a brief...."

Several law courses will do that, she thought.

"Can I ask why you're temping?"

The question came up once in a while, but never this early in a job. It threw her a little. "Oh, ah...I like the flexibility. If I don't want to work, I don't have to."

"I take it you have a husband."

She looked at him, puzzled. "Why would you think that?"

"Because you have to have another source of income since you couldn't possibly get a steady one from your temp job. Husbands usually provide that. So do you have a husband?''

She laughed. ''No. No husband.''

He smiled a gorgeous smile. He could kill a woman with that smile, she thought. Then he frowned. Even that was cute, too. ''The temp agency must pay very well then.''

She chuckled. ''From your mouth to God's ear. Actually, no. Although they charge you guys a fortune for me.''

He grinned wryly. ''I wish I could charge it back to Elise, my former secretary, for dumping me this way.''

''I never feel guilty for leaving a job early,'' Alison commented. ''That's the beauty of this. If I don't like a job or I need to move on, then I just call the agency and they put someone else in. This way no one loses.''

Which was why she used a temp agency when she scoped out an area for the witness-protection program. She got to see what kind of jobs were available for those who needed new lives. It also allowed her to get a feel for the people in an area. She found it most effective, certainly more so than sitting in a regional office and reading a newspaper to get the details. Besides, the protection program preferred to operate separately from the rest of the bureau, for security reasons.

''But you don't make money if you don't work,'' he said.

''Money's not everything,'' she replied blithely.

''Try telling that to the IRS.''

She laughed.

''You don't have job security, either,'' he continued. ''Or career advancement.''

''Career advancement is overrated,'' she told him. ''And I've got more security than twenty-year career people these days. I can get another job the next day. People dumped out have to go through the hiring process, which can be very long and painful.''

"You're a real free spirit, aren't you?" he asked.

She shrugged. "Sounds like it. I guess if I walk like a duck and talk like a duck, I must be a duck."

Of course, she couldn't explain to him about her real job, or that she'd joined the FBI because her real father had been witness to Mafia embezzling and had been killed after testifying. Her birth mother had put Alison up for adoption shortly afterward. She couldn't further explain her own sense of justice or her need to ensure that the program, in place after her birth father's death, would work for others who needed it. And she couldn't explain that being in this end of the program satisfied a gypsy urge she had to travel the country. She'd seen a lot of it before landing in Philadelphia for a "hide in plain sight" plan.

"Oh, yeah. I'm a free spirit." She chuckled at the irony. No one was more committed to a job than she. She went beyond the job description to perform it.

"You interested at all in a permanent job?" he asked.

The look in his eyes made her pause in answering. She had the feeling he was asking about more than a job. Shaking off the strange notion, she said, "Not me."

He opened his mouth to say something, but the entrance doors swung wide and a young woman strode in. "Hi, guys. How we doing here? Wow! Music and everything. This office sounds perky, a miracle."

"Hi, E.J.," Jared said, turning away from Alison. "This is Alison Palmer from Tempmates. Alison, this is Elizabeth Jane Spano, our office manager. She prefers E.J."

E.J. was Alison's age, about thirty, and plump with

dark hair and glasses. She had a combination adolescent and drill-sergeant look to her. E.J. offered her hand, and Alison shook it. E.J. said, "Hi. You're a peach for coming in on a holiday weekend, especially an end-of-summer one as gorgeous as this. I would have called and told this guy where to stick it. He couldn't pay me enough. It's beautiful outside."

"So why are you here?" Jared asked, exasperation in his voice.

"Hey, you're gonna pay me big-time for this, believe me." E.J. grinned. "I do the payroll. How's it going, Alison? You finding your way around or has this big dope totally confused you?"

"It's been fine," Alison said, not sure what to make of this whirlwind. But she kind of liked E.J.

"Hey! This 'dope' pays your salary," Jared complained.

"The *firm* pays my salary, of which you are a member."

"A voting one. You want to be a little nicer around the new person? I'd like to keep her for the duration."

"There are no clients here, so I insult with impunity." E.J. chuckled. "You don't pay me for my attitude, remember? Just my aptitude."

"Thank God."

"Besides, who would take the job?" E.J. leaned toward Alison. "They had ten different office managers in little more than a year before I came along."

"It was a nightmare," Jared said. "E.J. knows she can mouth off on me all she wants. As long as she stays."

"Jared and I get along just fine." E.J. smiled in satisfaction. She picked up one of the briefs Alison had already completed. After flipping through the first pages, she said, "These are good, Alison. Want a job?"

"No, thanks," Alison said, chuckling as she began working again.

"I already asked her," Jared said.

E.J. laughed. "Now, why am I not surprised?"

Alison flushed. Her reaction was silly, she knew. Yet the damn blush happened automatically.

"E.J., go home," Jared said.

"You are a brilliant man. I need a few things from my desk first, and then I'm off to a picnic with Nick's family. Maybe I'd be better off working."

E.J. strolled away.

Jared shook his head. "She's something."

Alison wondered why he put up with the woman's attitude, aptitude notwithstanding. The ten prior managers probably had something to do with it. She also wondered what the rest of the staff would be like. She'd find out tomorrow.

"I better get back to work," Jared said, after watching her type for a few moments. "If you need anything, just come get me."

Not if I can help it, she thought, although she only said, "OK."

He stood for a moment longer. Alison had the urge to stop typing and kiss him. Now that was a ludicrous thought. She fought to keep her composure from slipping.

Finally, he walked away. His office door shut and she slumped. She let out a sigh of relief.

She'd better get her mind on her job. Both jobs. The sooner she was out of here, the better.

JARED LOOKED UP from tomorrow's opening argument notes when E.J. knocked and poked her head in his door.

"Hey, boss man. The nicest one of them," she said, coming into his office. She shut the door behind her. "So how is Alison? Think you can live with her for a week?"

"I think I can live with her forever," Jared said, half-serious. "If you like her, offer her Elise's old job."

"She looks like an Earth Child, hardly a legal secretary," E.J. commented.

"She was told casual for today. Hell, E.J., nobody's here. And look at you. You've got on a T-shirt that says My Husband's Other Wife Is Normal, a pair of raggedy shorts and orthopedic sandals."

"It's Labor Day, and I've got a picnic to go to." She grinned. "I was just testing you, the original button-down man. But she better look more the image tomorrow or it'll be a short week. Meantime, let's see how she does. The last two temps who came in didn't make it through the third day. If she lasts past that, then we'll marry her, OK?"

Jared grinned. If only E.J. knew how close to the mark she was over his initial silly reaction to Alison Palmer. "OK. But she's good, and she's efficient. I wouldn't be in this position if Elise had been efficient. I can't believe those briefs weren't already filed with the court. They have to be in tomorrow or I'll have to wait for the next month's docket."

"I know. I love Nick to distraction, but I've always gotten my work done," E.J. said. She and her husband had gotten married last fall. "But wait until Robert gets in tomorrow. Once Alison gets a load of our illustrious head of the firm, she may run for the hills, and I wouldn't blame her."

"You handle Robert just fine." Jared chuckled. Robert Davis, son of one of the founders of Davis, Hansen and Davis, was a fussy, contrary, demanding man who believed in employee intimidation to get production results. E.J. had taken the bully by the horns on nearly her first day and hadn't yet let go. It was fun to watch her in action.

"I'm off," E.J. said. "But we know that. Try not to work so hard. Do you ever go home, Jared? Hit on a woman once in a while? Sleep with a client? Anything that says you're human and not a workaholic?"

Jared shrugged. "Not if I can help it. E.J., you know they're going to open a senior partnership soon. I've worked for it ever since I got here as a law clerk. I have plenty of time for marriage. No need to rush the process."

"You'll be a lonely, old, rude noise before you know it, Jared Holiday." She opened the door. "And I wasn't talking about marriage, I was talking about sex. Have some. You'll feel better."

She left him to it.

Jared sighed and studied his notes—or tried to. Somehow he couldn't concentrate. Odd images of Alison sifted through his brain, combining with E.J.'s advice about sex.

"Coffee," he muttered. He needed coffee to clear his head.

He went into the kitchen through the back hallway, avoiding the main work area. Avoiding Alison. He'd been tested enough today. Maybe he ought to rethink his conversation with E.J. Alison might be good and efficient, but she'd sent his senses into a major tailspin the few times he'd been in her presence.

Stress. He was experiencing stress for the first time in

his life. Normally, he thrived on the sixty-hour work weeks and critical situations in which he had to perform well. All of that was bound to catch up.

"Hell, I'm thirty-six," he muttered, thinking that was an age where catching up was bound to start.

He'd just poured coffee in his cup when Alison walked into the room. He swung around, knowing who it was. She paused on the threshold, looking like a freckle-faced angel. Stress slammed into him like an eighteen wheeler moving at eighty miles an hour.

"Did I startle you?" she asked, coming farther into the kitchen.

What an understatement, he thought, while saying inanely, "I was just getting coffee."

"Oh. I thought I'd take a break. It's noon."

Jared glanced at the clock. "That's fine."

She smiled, a flash of playfulness on her face. "My stomach thanks you."

"You're welcome."

She brushed past him to refill her pot with water, leaving behind a wisp of delicate perfume. She could drive a sober man to drink. Every one of Jared's nerve endings was on red alert. Her lips looked so kissable that he wanted to taste them...to feel them open under his own.

He realized he couldn't kiss her. Worse, he couldn't ask her out after work. He couldn't say a word to her on any level outside of business. This was her first day.

In point of fact, he couldn't date her the entire time she worked at the firm. If he opened his mouth once, she'd probably call the harassment cops, and he wouldn't blame her one bit.

But God knows, he wanted to do all those things. And more.

"E.J. suggested I take my lunch whenever I wanted. Is that a problem?"

"No problem," he said. "No problem at all."

Liar.

Chapter Two

Alison took a deep breath, smoothed down the pleat in her skirt and opened the doors of Davis, Hansen and Davis. Yesterday she hadn't been nervous at all. Today she was. She didn't have to look far to figure out why.

Jared Holiday.

"May I help you?" the receptionist asked, glancing up from a madly ringing phone system. Yesterday the phones had been silent.

"I'm the temp for Jared Holiday."

"You are?" The receptionist stared at her in surprise. "I didn't know he needed one."

"He did after Elise eloped and quit," Alison said, figuring she wasn't telling the woman anything new.

"She did? Nobody tells me anything."

"Oops," Alison muttered, feeling as though she was gossiping.

"Alison! Thanks, Mary." E.J. bustled up to her. The office manager looked positively conservative in a green suit. Or maybe it was blue. Alison was glad she'd worn her black, knee-length skirt and a simple white blouse. Safe colors for her, since she was one of the few women who were color-blind. Not severely, but some greens and reds tended to blend together on her and some blues never quite showed up in her repertoire. Yesterday's dress was easy, being one piece, but the mixing and matching could be disastrous. Clothing, unfortunately, lacked luminosity, which was the biggest clue to shadings. Color blindness was another reason she had the job she had with the bureau. She couldn't give totally accurate descriptions of clothing, eye color and such.

E.J. took her arm and dragged her back to the working area. "God, what a morning. I hate the holidays."

"I'm sorry I'm late, but the traffic was awful on the 676," Alison apologized, knowing she should have arrived fifteen minutes ago.

"The Blue Route's always awful. Don't worry about it. Look, I'm going to need you to take those briefs you typed yesterday to the court for Jared to file. The person who usually does it just called in sick. From the shore, no doubt."

"No problem. I have one more to finish and pack up."

"Great. Just get over there by noon, when court breaks for lunch. Jared will be waiting for you outside Judge Butkowski's court. Room 143."

"E.J., my mail is not on my desk."

E.J. turned, taking Alison with her. They faced a tall man in his fifties, wearing a black suit and school tie. His gaze could have cut ice. Alison felt raked as he glanced at her. He looked unlikable.

"The mail hasn't come yet, Robert," E.J. said, her voice cool.

"Oh." The winds went out of his sails. "Well, what about Saturday's?"

"We asked the post office to hold over all Saturday mail until the next working day because you felt we were having pieces stolen out of our mailbox on the weekends."

"That's right. Make sure I get my mail as soon as it comes in."

"I'll get it to you as soon as I can, Robert," E.J. said sweetly.

Robert's gaze settled fully on Alison. "Who's this?"

Alison resisted the urge to answer, "The man in the moon." She had been out of bureau discipline for years, and it showed.

"Alison Palmer. She's temping for Jared. Alison, this is Robert Davis, head of the firm."

"Hello," Alison said, smiling. She extended her hand.

Davis looked at it for a long moment, then shook it briefly. "Hello." His voice grew colder when he turned to E.J. "Why wasn't I told about this? And where's Elise?"

"Elise quit to elope with that rich guy she was dating."

"Elope!"

"Yes, elope. Friday." E.J. snorted. "When you were out on an extended weekend, which is why I haven't been able to tell you until now."

"Oh."

Alison smothered a broader smile. E.J. seemed to let this guy walk into every trap, then she pulled the rug out from under him. Alison had a whole new respect for the woman.

"I need some files, E.J.—"

"You have a secretary, Robert, and she's very capable of getting them, I'm sure. Certainly she'd do it a whole lot faster than I could, because I have to run the office like I'm paid to do."

E.J. took Alison toward Jared's office area, leaving the head of the firm behind them.

"He's a pain in the ass," E.J. said. "Pardon my

French, but he is. If he asks you to do something for him, just come to me and I'll tell you how or have someone else take it, if you're busy with Jared's work."

"OK." Alison hoped she didn't have to deal with Robert Davis while she was here.

"See me before you're ready to go over to the courthouse. I'll give you directions. It'll take you about a half hour."

Alison nodded. After E.J. left her, she settled in at her desk, then went in search of water to heat her tea. She needed tea to function. Several people, mostly women, were in the kitchen getting coffee. One or two smiled and said hello. The others ignored her, a typical happening in Alison's temp experience. But it gave her another clue on whether witnesses would find anonymity easy in their new home, or whether they would have to deal with overly friendly people.

A couple of the older women looked askance at her, especially her hair, which was pulled back from her face and left to hang free. Alison knew the style enhanced her free-spirit image and that was fine with her. She hated wearing her hair up, since it made her look like a kid playing at Grace Kelly. These people were more uptight than a graduating class at the academy. And that was uptight.

She was used to the coolness, however. Most temps received it wherever they went. But it helped to distance one from the office politics, the pecking order and the gossip.

Back at her desk, she glanced at Jared's shut door. Yesterday felt like a surreal dream—especially her reaction to him. Despite the elevator music droning through the area, she managed to quickly finish and package up the last brief. She also took several calls from hostile-sounding women upset that Jared was at court. Getting directions from E.J., she headed for the courthouse. Traffic was again a nightmare. She made several notes, knowing that settling someone in this area could leave them with problems getting around.

The Chester County Courthouse was a typical low, squat building with modern lines and nothing to set itself apart from other county courthouses across the country. Alison found the judge's court without trouble. Room 143 was still in session. She sat down on a bench outside the closed doors and leaned her head against the wall. The pile of envelopes sat on her lap. She kept one arm over them, securing the stack.

Interesting job so far, she admitted wryly. She now knew the domestic mishaps of strangers' lives, and travel was included. What more could a person ask for?

The doors suddenly swung open with a bang. A man stormed out, followed by another carrying a briefcase and bleating about not being told something. Several other people filed out. Finally, Jared emerged.

Alison felt that jolt of sensuality shoot through her in a replay of yesterday. He looked sensational in a gray— she was positive about grays—pinstriped suit. If Philadelphia lawyers were sharks, then she wanted to be eaten up by Jared.

A woman who had to be wearing a designer dress, since the thing fit her slim body like a glove, came out behind him and clutched his arm. Jealousy swept through Alison.

"You were wonderful, Jared," the woman said, batting her eyelashes at him. "David thought he could get away with not disclosing that account you ferreted out."

Jared patted her hand. "I'm here to fight for you, Barbara. Women have rights in a marriage and divorce, and

they're entitled to all the benefits those rights guarantee.''

"But I wouldn't have known about the extra money
without you as my lawyer. Let me buy you lunch today.''

"I wish I could, but I have other papers to file now
for other women in trouble." Jared smiled at Alison,
whose heart thumped wildly. The jealousy vanished with
his attention.

This man was making her crazy, she thought.

"I understand," the woman said, her gaze worshipful.

Alison wondered whether he took advantage of
women like this one, who had stars in their eyes about
him. She hoped he did and hoped he didn't. The first
because she needed something to dislike about him, and
the second because the first would be despicable. She'd
not like to think he was despicable.

"Hi," Jared said to her, after saying goodbye to his
client.

"Hi," Alison said shyly, rising to her feet.

The briefs tumbled to the floor.

Her face heated as Jared bent down with her to pick
the folders up. At least they didn't clunk heads. But how
obvious could she be?

"Doesn't this only happen in the movies?" she mum-
bled, feeling like the stereotypical klutz with the leading
man.

"Depends on the movie." Jared grinned at her.

"Somehow I knew you'd say that." She had. The
notion sobered her, banishing the playful moment. She
straightened after Jared took half the load from her.

"We need to see Judge Butkowski's clerk." He led
her back into the courtroom. A young, black woman,

who reminded Alison of E.J. somehow, greeted him from behind a counter.

"Back again to cut the legs out of some poor slob?"

Boy, was she E.J., Alison thought with a grin.

"Yolanda, you have no heart," Jared replied.

"Hey, why should I? The women were stupid enough to marry the jerks in the first place, why should they crucify them now?" Yolanda eyed Alison. "Who's the pretty lady? Don't tell me you finally got a girlfriend. Way to go, Mr. H."

Alison flushed, a chronic condition with this man. Her face was so hot she must be beet red. At least she wouldn't be able to ever see how bad it looked.

But now she knew he wasn't married.

"No, Yolanda. You have put your foot in it, as usual. This is Alison, a temp who's working for me. Elise quit. She eloped over the weekend."

"She'll be in here by Christmas. As your client," Yolanda predicted. She grinned at Alison. "Honey, you're too good for this man, anyway. Everyone is. Here, let me take those."

"Thanks." Alison handed over her stack, as did Jared, who grumbled about Yolanda's comment. Clearly, he liked this woman who teased him unmercifully. It said a lot that he took it in stride.

"Presents for the judge," Yolanda mused. She made a face. "Just what he loves. More work. All for next month's docket?"

Jared nodded. "Please. They have to get on there."

"You cut it close."

"I wouldn't have cut it at all if Alison hadn't come in yesterday and put them together for me." He smiled gratefully at her.

Alison's heart melted.

"Anyone named Holiday who makes a person work on a holiday ought to be shot," Yolanda pronounced.

"As long as he pays me," Alison quipped. This one had the same no-nonsense attitude as E.J.

"I like this girl," Yolanda said. "She's got her priorities straight. Now go away. It's my lunch hour in two minutes."

They left Yolanda clucking over the briefs.

Outside the courtroom, Jared said, "Come on. I'll take you to lunch."

Alison hesitated. Lunch felt fraught with crevices and precipices, not as simple as it seemed.

"I owe you for giving up a holiday to work," he continued, smiling that smile that somehow made her melt inside. He added, "Besides, who's going to yell? I'm the boss."

Alison smiled back. "Good point."

"That's what I thought." Jared grinned.

SITTING ACROSS from Alison at Sam's Deli felt right...easy and yet intriguing. The booth kept a fair distance between them. Jared wished he'd taken a small table so their legs could bump accidentally. Maybe that wasn't a healthy idea. He watched her tuck into a Reuben sandwich, fascinated with every movement she made. So much so that his heart beat slightly faster and his blood pressure was definitely elevated. He really had to get checked out.

He decided to hell with his body. He could watch Alison forever. She just looked so ethereal with her long hair left free down her back. Viking princess. Celtic sorceress. She held an ancient, almost mythical air.

She grinned around her sandwich bite. "I know this

is a heart attack on rye bread, but what the heck. I'll work it off later. I hope."

"You work out?" he asked, curious about her life. "What do you do? Run? Bike?"

He could swear she looked nonplussed, an odd response for someone who'd brought up the subject. She finally replied, "I run and bike. When I can. In-line skate. All sorts of sports. What about you?"

"I watch what I eat and walk the treadmill every morning…if I can," he admitted, looking glumly at his salad plate with low-fat dressing.

She must have caught his wistfulness for she said, "I promise not to tell if you trade that salad in for a sub."

He grinned. "Don't tempt me."

She shrugged and took another bite of her packed sandwich, torturing him.

Her tone had a slight accent he couldn't place. He hadn't noticed yesterday, his mind too full of her total impact to take in many details. His reaction was under a little better control now. Between her underlying twang and calling a hoagie a sub, she definitely hadn't grown up in Philadelphia. "Where are you from?"

She paused. "Wayne."

He chuckled, Wayne being a town down the road. "I live in Bryn Mawr, but I didn't mean your current home. I can tell you're not from Philly."

"Why would you say that?" she asked, her sandwich frozen in midair.

"Because your accent isn't right and you called it—" he gestured toward her sandwich "—a sub, not a hoagie."

"Oh." She shrugged again and took another bite. "Mmm, but this is good."

"You're going to torture me with that, aren't you?" His salad looked less appealing than ever.

"We all make choices in life," she told him, her blue eyes sparkling with humor and mischief. "Yours was salad."

He snagged the waitress. "I'm making a new choice in life. Get me a hoagie, please."

The girl arched her eyebrows. "Something wrong with the salad?"

"No, except it's not a hoagie." He smiled at her. "I've decided I can't handle rabbit food today, after all."

The waitress chuckled. "I've had days like that, too. I'll get you a hoagie. American or Italian?"

"Italian. If I'm going to live, I might as well do it dangerously." The waitress whisked away the forlorn salad plate. Jared turned to Alison, who had grinned through the entire exchange. "Want a running partner tonight?"

"Running partner? Oh. Sorry, you're on your own."

"Thanks. First you encourage me to sin, then you turn me away from the penance."

She laughed.

"So how did you become a divorce lawyer?" she asked.

"I went to law school."

"OK. I deserve that one. Did you know you wanted to do divorce work from the start?"

"No. I wanted to make the big bucks in corporate law." His hoagie arrived, its promptness as well as its luscious meats and cheeses eliciting a moan of satisfaction from Jared. "Ahh...now this is a thing of beauty, a joy forever, better than diamonds.... Look at this roll. Have you ever seen a more beautiful roll?"

"Not in my lifetime," Alison said.

"Me, neither. It's the queen of rolls. And the salami smells splendid, loaded with garlic."

"Better take a breath mint afterward."

"I'll need two, I'm sure. The provolone is that wonderful white-yellow only possible from the freshest of goat milk. Or is it cow?"

Alison coughed delicately. "I think it's bull."

Jared leaned across the booth. "I think you're right. But let's not forget the crisp tomatoes, the paper-thin slices of onions and the delicately shredded lettuce. They all combine for enough calories to last the rest of the week."

"Bon appetit," Alison replied.

"I thank you." He took a bite of his hoagie. The tanginess of the cappicola ham and Genoa salami, the sharpness of the cheese, the juiciness of the tomatoes and the crunchiness of the onions and lettuce combined to intoxicate his palate. "Damn, but that's wicked. Very wicked and very good."

Alison laughed. "Enjoy. For tomorrow we fast."

"Got it in one." He savored his hoagie, then said, "Where were we? Oh, yes, my detour into divorce law. Frankly, I started clerking at Davis, Hansen and Davis for corporate, but an opening came in the divorce side, and I jumped at it, thinking I'd just get my feet wet with some actual practice. I found I was good at it, so I stayed." He grinned. "I'm making more than corporate lawyers my age. The bottom dropped out of that side a few years back."

"So you like it and the money's good?"

"Yes. I like helping people, too. Many times, people get back together rather than get divorced. I make very sure they have no other alternative before we proceed in court.''

He left his explanation at that, although he wanted to explain more. He'd found his niche in helping women further back than a change in law practice. Years ago, when he'd been a kid, his grandmother had had an affair. Jared hadn't blamed his grandmother one bit, at the time, although everyone else in the family did. His grandfather had been a domineering, critical man who was never happy with anything his wife did. His grandfather had treated others, including Jared, well enough, but Jared had noticed the difference during the summers he'd spent at his grandparents' shore home. Jared's cousins, Peter, Michael and Raymond, hadn't seemed to care about how their grandmother was being treated. But he had loved his grandmother dearly, and his grandfather's constant picking bothered him. No wonder she turned to someone kinder.

That summer, when Jared had been twelve, he had seen the aftermath when his grandmother's affair was discovered. He would never forget coming upon his Nan, crying. She had wept on Jared's adolescent shoulders and begged his forgiveness. Of course, he'd forgiven her. She was his Nan. She had told him he would understand one day when he looked at someone and fell in love. Only the man hadn't fallen in love with his grandmother in turn—and that was the tragedy.

Jared had scoffed at love at first sight after that. The emotion had ruined his grandmother. She had nearly succeeded in taking her life and never was the same after that.

He'd scoffed until Alison...

Forget it, he told himself. All his experience made an extremely good case for gonads at first sight, not love.

Love at first sight simply didn't exist. But he really
ought to have his heart tested. It had begun doing crazy
flip-flops again, the moment he'd seen her after court
adjourned, and they still hadn't stopped.

"I probably ought to get back," Alison said, finishing
the last of her lunch. "E.J. must be wondering where I
got to."

"Wait until I'm finished," he said, not willing to let
her go just yet. He and she had had a nice lunch thus
far. They'd talked together easily, establishing a rapport.
Besides, he loved just looking at her. Although she was
dressed more conservatively today, her curves beckoned
for his touch. And he wanted to touch them. Every one
of them. "Don't worry about E.J. Just tell her I bought
you lunch at Sam's. In fact, I'm heading back to the
office, too, so I'll tell her myself."

She smiled. "Thanks. And thanks for lunch."

"Thank you. You saved me from angry clients. I hate
angry clients."

They departed shortly after that in their separate cars.
Alison drove a two-seater, late-model Fiero. Her choice
of car surprised Jared. An old VW bug seemed more her
type.

He felt really good about Alison. He bet if he dragged
out his old list, she would already have a number of
positives on it. But he would take this day by day—an
alien action for a man who planned every event of his
life well in advance of it happening.

He realized she had never told him where she was
originally from. He'd have to ask again.

He lost Alison in traffic and when he reached the
firm's parking lot, he noticed she'd beat him in. Not only
did he need a checkup, but it seemed his "Beamer" did,
too.

Inside the office, he found Alison being dressed down by Robert.

"...You people are incredibly unreliable," Robert was saying, glaring at Alison, who stood quietly before the man. Being bombastic was Robert's favorite pastime, and he had a victim. E.J. was nowhere around, although the rest of the office looked on gleefully. "It's ridiculous what we get sent that's supposed to pass for competent help! What's your name again—"

"Alison Palmer," Jared interjected, getting within speaking distance. "She was with me at the courthouse, Robert. E.J. sent her over with papers I had to file today, and I took her to lunch afterward. We're both just getting back." Jared glanced at his watch. "It's only a little more than ninety minutes since she left here."

Robert's face turned bright red. Jared didn't bother to muster any sympathy, since the man brought on his own embarrassment. Alison, taking advantage of the situation, slipped past Robert without a word and went to her desk. E.J. had warned about Alison getting a load of Robert in action. Jared had hoped it wouldn't be this soon.

"Why don't I know anything that goes on here?" Robert asked.

Jared resisted the urge to tell him he was a pain in the ass who worried over nonsense. Instead he took an E.J. tack. "Robert, you have enough to do without being bothered by little things such as when a temp leaves and returns from lunch or errands. Hell, man, that's what we have E.J. for."

"I just didn't know why the temp was coming in late," Robert said, whining.

"I'll take care of Alison, OK?" Jared caught himself hoping the words were prophetic.

"Fine, but see that she does her work. I'm tired of paying people for nothing."

There were about three more people job hunting just to get away from Robert's public outbursts, Jared thought. He wondered why he put up with Robert, then wondered how many times he'd wondered that. In the billions by now. He must be neck and neck with the hamburgers McDonald's had sold over the years. Davis, Hansen and Davis paid extremely well, the big plus. Robert, however, was becoming a bigger minus all the time.

After leaving Robert to contemplate his navel, an impossible wish, Jared went straight to Alison at her desk. "I apologize for that."

"Why? You did nothing wrong, and neither did I." She smiled, looking perfectly carefree. "So do I pack my stuff?"

"Hell, no. I need you."

The statement meant far more than work, and he knew it. She looked at him oddly, as if she sensed the same. His whole reaction to her was simply unexplainable. One look and he was a goner, it seemed.

He looked at her tote bag to distract himself. Curious, he asked, "What do you have in there, anyway? Or should I not ask?"

"You can." She grinned and opened the tote. "I have my little teapot, my tea, some fruit for snacks, a radio, the daily newspapers and a book."

"Really? Why all that?"

"I never know what I'm walking into on a job, so I carry everything. This way, if I'm just baby-sitting phones, I have something to read. On jobs like this I don't need the tote, but I like to be prepared. Probably tomorrow I won't bring all this."

Under the fairy-princess look was an efficient woman, in her own way. He had a feeling she held many more contradictions.

"As long as you're coming back tomorrow. Again, I am sorry you were subjected to Robert. He's...never mind what he is. Don't worry about him again. I'll handle Robert."

Jared reached out to pat her arm in reassurance—or meant to. But she turned suddenly, putting her breast right where her arm had been a second before.

Yanking his hand away as if it had been burned, Jared registered sixty things at once. Shock, horror and delight vied for the biggest slots. His heart pounded, his body shook and his blood raced uncontrollably. He thought for a moment that he would actually pass out. A part of his brain noted her breast fit his palm perfectly, the small globe seemingly made for him. His mouth apologized profusely for this new faux pas. "I'm sorry. I—I meant to touch your arm...I wasn't trying to do anything—"

"It's OK," Alison said, although her face was bright red. "I know it was an accident."

She looked past him toward the rest of the office. Her frantic expression eased. Jared wanted to turn but was afraid he'd attract more attention than they already might have.

"Did anyone notice?" he asked.

"I don't think so."

"Alison, I am really sorry—"

"It's OK."

He didn't know what else to say without making a bad situation worse. He escaped to his office and shut the door behind him. So much for making strides during lunch. He'd just slid right back to square one, if not worse.

His heart began pounding again. His body trembled and his mind replayed that moment over and over. In all his career, he had never groped an employee, accidentally or otherwise.

He half hoped it would happen again.

Now that kind of thinking had to stop, he told himself. He was a grown man who needed to be in control of his feelings. He was a businessman of sorts, a professional. He *was* in control.

That evening, he sat on the padded bench and tried to ignore the cold, round disk against his bare chest. Never had he felt more out of control.

"Breathe out," his doctor ordered.

Jared breathed out.

Dave thumped his chest, then straightened. "You sound good, Jared. Your stress test looks fine and your blood pressure is within normal limits. You're in good shape."

Jared wasn't sure if he were happy or disappointed with Dave's pronouncement. He voted for disappointed. Something physically wrong would explain a lot.

Now he was back to square one in the Alison-reaction department.

"I just wanted to be sure," he said. "It's been awhile since my last physical."

"You sounded desperate on the phone."

"Yes, well…" He shrugged. He'd avoided Alison for the rest of the afternoon, but his body hadn't recovered from the inadvertent, intimate touch.

"You probably just need to take it easy at work," Dave said. "That's where stress often comes from. If you've got vacation time, it wouldn't hurt to take it."

No kidding, Jared thought. Unfortunately, he didn't

have time for a vacation. He still couldn't believe the blooper he'd committed today.

"I'll try," he said half-heartedly, while hopping off the table.

Well, one explanation for his reaction was down the tubes. The other one scared him.

Maybe after what had happened today, Alison Palmer wouldn't return to Davis, Hansen and Davis.

He didn't know what to do if she didn't.

Chapter Three

Alison sat down at the desk and wondered why she had come back to Davis, Hansen and Davis.

She had never left a job before it was finished, for one thing, having timed them to end with her real job. For another, not coming back seemed like running away from what had been an accidental touch. Heck, she was at as much fault as Jared. Third...

She had no third.

What she did have was only three days to go, and she'd be out of here forever. Out of contact with Jared Holiday. That suited her. Her breast still burned from his touch.

So why did she have this funny, empty feeling at the thought of not seeing him again?

Better not analyze it, she decided. Better to just let it be. The Beatles knew what they were talking about.

"Good morning."

Jared's voice reached her before his body did. Startled, Alison wondered where her normally sensitive awareness had got to. It wasn't on the job, that was for sure. She turned her head, while keeping her body in place, wanting no "accidents" this time.

"Good morning," she said as cheerfully as she could,

trying to ignore the jolt that shot through her. How the hell did he manage that?

Jared smiled at her. "I'm glad you're here."

Alison swallowed. He sounded so seductive. This man managed a lot of things.

"I have a client coming in this afternoon after court for her first interview," he said, mercifully getting straight to business. "Do you take dictation?"

"No. Just dictaphone work."

"That's OK. E.J. usually sits in on these, but she'll be at the dentist this afternoon. I want you to take notes, and shorthand would be easier for you but it's not necessary."

"I write very fast when I have to." Alison smiled, relaxing a little. "I may not be able to tell you what it says afterward, but it'll be fast."

He grinned in return. "We'll work on that. Now, I have to go to court this morning. E.J. will send you over later with some things for me again. I'll buy you another lunch. I feel like I owe you one."

"Today's a fast day for me," she said, grateful that it was.

Jared's mouth dropped open. "A what?"

"A fast day," she repeated. "One day I eat whatever I want, then the next day I fast. Well, I eat only fruits and vegetables, but I call it a fast."

"You're kidding."

"No." She pushed a wandering hank of hair back off her shoulder. "It's not a method I'd recommend to everyone, but it works for me. I feel really good."

With her erratic life-style, she really didn't exercise regularly as she had implied yesterday. She'd found her every-other-day fruit binge the best way to maintain her

FBI weight, a requirement of the job whenever she went
back to Quantico for the annual refresher course.

"Well, you look..." He paused, chagrin easy to read
on his face. Obviously, he wasn't going down any physical road. She couldn't blame him, preferring herself to
act as if their bodies simply didn't exist.

She wished it was simple, her "nonexistent" body
ever aware of how good he looked. Right now, the man
could make *GQ* with that dark blue, or possibly green,
suit.

Maybe she was reading his response wrong today. He
might not like her beige dress. Maybe he stared at her
because the dress's short sleeves and fitted waist were
too risqué for Davis, Hansen and Davis. Maybe she
shouldn't care what he thought of her clothes.

"We'll do lunch another time then."

"Sure."

Meaningless words. He left her, going into his office
and ending her torment.

Alison slumped in her chair and sighed. Their first
meeting, after touch, could have been worse.

Jared came out of his office. Alison shot back up,
alert.

He handed her a huge pile of opened mail. "Type up
a thank-you or a reply letter to all these. I wrote my
answer on the top, just fill it out with politeness. Most
are straightforward, and you shouldn't have a problem.
Anything you're unsure of, just leave until I can go over
them with you. Sure you won't eat lunch today?"

She chuckled. "I'm sure. Sorry."

"Every other day, eh?"

"Every other."

"I bet you know your fruit."

"From the kiwi to the plantain. They are my friends."

"Damn." He shuddered, fruit clearly not a friend to him.

She just laughed.

He headed for court shortly after that. Alison felt a little better about her decision to finish the temp job here. Jared was still disconcerting, but they had reached beyond the awful awkwardness.

E.J. caught up with her about midmorning. The woman had apologized for Robert Davis's behavior yesterday, after she'd heard about it. Apologizing for the head of the firm must be an occupational hazard. Alison hadn't been bothered too much by the man's ranting. Occasionally, she had been subjected to nasty bosses before. The nice part about temp jobs was that one always knew the job was short and therefore one had an out with a bad boss. Also, the temp agency usually saw a pattern with companies and knew when one was being sent into the lion's den.

"Here's the stuff Jared needs," E.J. said, handing over some folders. "Take as long as you like. Go shopping at Nordstrom's. Get ice cream at Baskin-Robbins. Try on shoes at the Moglio boutique. It will serve Robert right after yesterday."

"Lucky for Mr. Davis, I'm too poor to shop this week," Alison said, grinning. E.J. was obviously teasing.

"Hell, honey, you don't have to *buy* anything. This is revenge shopping, the best kind." E.J. laughed at her own joke, then said, "Actually, I did that one afternoon when he ticked me off good. Then I marched into his office and read him the riot act. But since you like me, I know you'll be back. Seriously, if you want to take an early lunch or a little extra time, don't worry about it."

"OK." Alison didn't bother to explain her eating habits to E.J. There was no need.

E.J. looked over at the pile of nice, neat replies clipped to Jared's letters. "These really look good. You got through them quickly."

"They weren't hard," Alison said. She really liked the woman and her easy-going attitude. People like E.J. were a pleasure to work for.

"Robert's secretary has an appointment for this afternoon, too, so I think I'll have you do his mail when you get back," E.J. commented. "He likes it logged in and put in a certain order in his mail pouch. It's not hard, and it would help me out."

"All right," Alison said, albeit reluctantly. "But Jared does want me to take notes with an appointment of his this afternoon."

E.J. wave a hand in dismissal. "Oh, that's no problem. You'll be finished with Robert's mail long before that."

"OK."

"You'll find Jared's meeting interesting." E.J. chuckled. It sounded wicked. "I'll be at the dentist's. Pooh."

Alison didn't like E.J.'s glee, but didn't fret about it. Suddenly, she had a full slate of work, which suited her fine. It gave her less time to daydream over her "boss."

She got to the courthouse in better time than the day before. Room 143 was becoming a familiar place. So was the bench outside it.

Jared emerged with another attractive woman. He must go home and give prayers of thanks to the work gods for his job, Alison thought in disgust.

Jared disentangled himself from his client and the inevitable lunch invitation. Alison decided she had a real cynical streak.

He smiled at Alison. "Great! You're here."

"I feel like I'm at my home away from home," she said, standing up and *not* dropping the folders this time.

"After a while it *will* be your home," he told her, making the folder hand-off without a fault today. "I'm here more than anywhere else. These guys have to go to Judge Marks's office. That's on the next floor."

They walked up the marble staircase to an identical courtroom. The clerk behind the counter, however, was older than her counterpart downstairs, and motherly looking. She gazed over half glasses with shrewd eyes.

"Good morning, Counselor. You have something for Judge Marks today?"

"Some depositions she requested, Jane." He handed over the folders. "Jane, this is Alison Palmer. She's temping for me. Elise eloped this weekend and quit."

"Tsk, tsk. The unfaithful hussy." Jane grinned. "She'll be your client before the year's out."

"That's what Yolanda said."

Jane laughed. "Brilliant minds think alike. Hi, Alison. Don't mind us. I tease Counselor Holiday unmercifully."

"And I take it, because Jane's terrific," Jared said warmly.

"Hello, Jane. It's a pleasure to meet you." Alison smiled at the woman and shook hands.

"So how are you doing over there at Davis, Hansen and Davis?" Jane asked.

"Fine. I think. Everyone's been nice and patient," Alison replied.

"E.J.'s a sweetie. Tell her I said hello."

"I will."

Meeting people like E.J., Yolanda and Jane was the pleasurable part of this job. They restored Alison's faith in mankind's courtesy—yet left her a little wistful for roots in her gypsy life. These women could easily be friends if she hadn't the job she did.

She glanced at Jared and her wistfulness turned to something more primitive. Alison pushed the thought aside.

As she and Jared walked out of the courthouse, he said, "Sure you don't want to eat lunch today?"

"I'm sure. But thanks." Alison tried to smile easily. "I'll see you back at the office, OK?"

"I guess."

He sounded disappointed. She tried not to put stock in that. What would be the point? Besides, his interest in her could only be temporary, and she had a hell of an ego to think he might want anything more. Since she preferred no physical or emotional entanglements, she had no interest.

Or shouldn't.

"Wait a minute. You do eat fruit today, right?"

"Yes," she said warily.

"Then you do eat." He took her arm. "I'll buy you a kiwi at Sam's."

"But I have my fruit," she protested, laughing.

"So I'll buy you water. Did anyone ever tell you you're eating like a prisoner?"

"That's bread and water."

"Oh, yeah. I forgot. Well, it's my turn to torture you with a great sandwich. Maybe you'll kick rabbit food for the day."

As he swept her along, Alison wondered how to object.

She wondered if she even wanted to.

"SO WHY HAVEN'T YOU laid down that apple and picked up the menu?"

Jared stared at Alison, in awe of her willpower when faced with a cheeseburger and fries, his choice for lunch. No one resisted cheeseburgers and fries, the all-American meal.

"Because my apple tastes great," she replied. "It's a Braeburn from New Zealand. Crisp, sweet, yet a little tart."

"Sounds like an '86 Bordeaux." He leaned forward. "Is that *all* you're going to eat?"

"No. I have some grapes for dessert."

"That's a cornucopia, not a tote bag you carry around." He leaned back and signaled the waitress. "Today is guilt day. Take away the burger and fries, give it to some poor, hungry soul and get me a chef's salad."

Alison laughed.

The waitress was the same one as yesterday. Picking up the plate, she said, "I've had days like that, too."

"You chicken," Alison told him after the waitress left. "I had my eyes all fooled that your lunch was really an eggplant moussaka. I hate eggplant."

"Your eyes are too pretty to fool." The words shot out before he could stop himself.

She froze in midbite.

"I'm sorry," he said, chagrined at stepping into disaster again. "I've said something absolutely improper, and being attracted to you is no excuse. When we get back to the office, I'll tell E.J. I stuck my foot clear in up to my neck. You won't get in any trouble for leaving the job early. I promise you. I'll make sure you're paid for the week, too. You shouldn't lose anything because I've been stupid."

She finished biting into her apple and chewed for a

long, interminable moment before swallowing. "Are you firing me?"

"Hell, no." He swallowed, too, without benefit of food. "I'm assuming you'd want to leave because I've been a jerk...and because of what happened yesterday...."

"Actually, I'm kind of flattered you think I have pretty eyes. Your immediately laying yourself on the sacrificial altar of bosses shows me you really didn't mean to harass me."

"What about the attraction?" Jared asked, wanting everything to be out in the open at this point.

She looked at him steadily. "I'm only here for two more days. It's not a problem."

He hated the sound of that. "I don't get involved with people I work with, clients or employees. Anyone at Davis, Hansen and Davis can tell you that."

"OK." She pursed her lips, unconsciously making them eminently kissable.

Jared gripped his pant legs. He'd just finished apologizing for doing something stupid, and he was ready to do something stupid again. Only kissing her was hardly stupid. Well, it was, but not from a physical standpoint.

His salad came finally, the service slower today. He dug into it, wanting something to distract him from the awkwardness between him and Alison. Today the salad actually appealed, since his appetite had gone from famished to vanished in one stupid remark.

"I think changing the subject would be a good idea," she said finally.

"Me, too." He thought of his ideal-mate list and an unanswered question came to mind. "So where are you from? We got sidetracked yesterday when that came up before."

To his surprise, she blushed. He wouldn't have thought the innocent question bothered her more than his personal remark about her eyes. Yet clearly it did.

"Mmm…Chicago, originally. I've moved around a lot."

"Was your father in the service?"

"No. Why would you think that?"

"Because you moved around a lot."

"Oh. No, it's me who's done the moving."

She didn't say anything more. All of Jared's instincts were to ferret out the rest of her life, yet he held himself back. He'd made enough stupid moves with this woman already. If she wanted to tell him more, she would have.

"How do you like Philadelphia?" he asked, positive this had to be an innocent question.

"Nice," she replied, clearly finding it innocent, too. "It's not what I expected."

"It's had a bad reputation for years, but the downtown's been renovated and the suburbs have always been great. Were you a legal secretary in Chicago?"

"Ah…yes."

"What firm? Maybe I know them."

"I worked for a temp agency there, too. Actually, I've done a lot of different jobs—secretary, store manager, decorating, accounting.… I haven't really stayed with any one job long."

"How old are you?" Jared asked, half-appalled by her litany. She sounded like someone with no focus in her life. He couldn't imagine not having career goals.

"Thirty." She grinned wryly. "I know I don't look it. People tell me that all the time. I think it's the freckles."

He clamped his lips over telling her how beautiful her

freckles were. But she was thirty and single and temping
for a living. How the heck did she survive?

"Can I ask why you haven't stayed with a job long?"
he asked. "Or is that an improper question?"

"I can choose to answer or not." She smiled and took
a last bite of her apple. "Well, I guess I haven't found
my niche yet. I'm in no hurry. I'm having fun."

Alison's view on work was free spirited, he thought.
Hell, everything about her was free spirited. In fact, even
her dress today looked more elegant than businesslike.
Not that he was complaining, but she was not a little-
blue-suit lady. She wasn't even close.

Yet what he'd seen so far of her work ethic indicated
a focused, dedicated woman. She might not be in a job
for long, but she threw herself into it while she was.

He wished he knew where she lived and other things
about her personal life. She intrigued him like no other
woman had in a long time.

He knew he should keep his distance physically and
conversationally, but he couldn't. He'd made an ass of
himself twice already, not the deterrent they should be
to his curiosity.

She was leaving in two days.

What would he do then?

"ALISON, I'm ready for you now."

Jared's head and shoulders vanished behind his office
door as suddenly as they had emerged. Alison blinked,
wondering if she had heard right. Her blood pulsed just
a little more eagerly. Yep, she *had* seen Jared in the
flesh. Not quite the flesh, she thought, but close enough.
And the notion that he was "ready" for her only got her
blood going more.

"Calm down, girl," she muttered, as she picked up a steno pad and pen. "He's got a client in there."

Still, as she walked to the office door, his accidental confession came to her mind. She didn't doubt it was an accident, since he'd been so defensively apologetic afterward. She didn't doubt she'd been captured by it, either.

Oh, brother, what a mess, she thought.

Inside his office, she found the client, another elegantly dressed and attractive woman, seated in one of the wing chairs before Jared's desk. Jared leaned against the edge of his desk, directly in front of the woman. They both looked up when Alison came in.

Innocent, she thought with relief, then wondered why she'd thought anything else at all. A small statue of Justice stood on Jared's desk. Her shapely figure and clinging gown looked more like an ad for a porn movie than a stern arbiter of right and wrong. In fact, the statue seemed to have a Mona Lisa smile.

Nah, she thought. She was seeing things now.

"Alison," Jared said, with something like relief in his voice as he straightened. "Alison, this is Mrs. Joan Markson. You'll be taking notes of this meeting for us."

Mrs. Markson frowned. "I'd rather not have an audience, Jared."

"Alison's not an audience," he assured her. He motioned Alison toward the other wing chair. "She's my secretary."

Alison slid into the chair as unobtrusively as she could. "Hello, Mrs. Markson."

The Markson woman said nothing for a moment, then sighed. "Oh, I don't care."

Alison smothered a smile. Usually when people objected to something, then said they didn't care, they did very much. Jared, however, wasn't budging.

"I'm glad you don't mind, because we couldn't do this without Alison here...."

Alison thought the statement interesting, since E.J. was originally supposed to be present.

"...Now, tell me why you want to divorce your husband," Jared continued, in a very gentle voice.

"He's gone too far," Joan Markson snapped, a catch in hers. "I've turned a blind eye for years at his affairs, but now he's got—" she glanced at Alison, then back to Jared "—he's got *two* women at once. Two!"

"Two women," Alison wrote dutifully on the note pad.

"It's disgusting!" Mrs. Markson went on. "He's a brain surgeon, for goodness sake. A respected member of the community. And he's fifty, bald and fat! He needs a brain implant. On himself!"

Alison bit her lip to keep from snorting in amusement. She wrote down "brain surgeon, fifty, bald and fat." She resisted the urge to add that Dr. Markson had one screw loose. Or maybe it was two.

"I'm humiliated!" Mrs. Markson wailed. "I know all my friends are laughing behind my back. I just know it."

Jared reached out and held Mrs. Markson's hand. "They should be in awe that it took *two* women to replace you."

"Really?" The woman sniffed back tears. "You think so?"

"I very much think so." With his free hand, Jared pulled a tissue out of a box on his desk, gave it to Mrs. Markson, then handed the box to Alison.

Alison took the box, realizing she had just been designated Keeper of the Kleenex. She pulled a second one out and immediately handed it over to the client, who looked ready for a spare.

"Thank you," Mrs. Markson said, dabbing her eyes with the new tissue.

The woman told her story, with fresh tears every so often. Her list of complaints and slights stretched through seven pages on the steno pad. By the time the woman was finished, Alison wondered why Mrs. Markson had ever married the crumb in the first place.

Amazingly, Jared was the model of sympathy. He treated his client like a wronged queen, coaxing and urging her story forward with common sense and tender words. When it was clear reconciliation would happen the same day hell froze over, he told her in varying ways that all men were bums and that he would extract justice on her behalf. Jared Holiday was a wonderful mix of hero, father and avenging angel. By the time the meeting was over, Mrs. Markson was half in love with him.

So was Alison.

Alison watched him with goo-goo eyes. She knew they were goo-goo. She couldn't help it. He was so sweet and so gentlemanly, no woman could imagine him with a single male failing. Couple the killer attitude with the killer face and body, and no woman could resist him. Mrs. Markson couldn't. The woman clung to him occasionally. He patted her back, then extricated himself in brotherly fashion.

Alison wanted to wrap her arms around him and say, "Take me. Take me now!" It was all she could do to sit in the damn chair and hand over tissues on command.

"I want George to pay." Joan Markson said, as Jared escorted her to the door. "I stood by him, but no more. I want everything, Jared. *Everything.*"

"I'll make sure you're happy, Joan. Very happy," Jared promised, waving Alison back in her chair when she rose to leave, too.

After he closed the door on the Markson interview, he let out his breath in relief and grinned. "Thanks. I hate doing these interviews alone."

"I guess so," Alison said, raising her eyebrows. "You must be unhappy hearing about what your half of the species does."

Jared laughed. "I guarantee you that Dr. Markson's lawyer is hearing about what your half of the species is capable of. That ain't pretty, either."

Alison grinned back and said wryly, "I guess not. What do you want done with the notes?"

"Nothing for now. I've taped the entire thing."

"You did? Then why was I here?"

"In case something goes wrong with the tape."

"That makes sense."

"And because women eventually open up more with another woman present. Remember, I'm from the bastard side of the species, so I might not initially appear sympathetic in their eyes."

"But you were the model of sympathy," Alison said.

"Thank you."

There was a knock on the door, then E.J. came in. "Sorry I wasn't here, Jared. Oh, good. Alison sat in for me. How did you like the client initial interview? The CII, as I call it. They're eye-openers."

"I feel like mine are wide," Alison admitted, chuckling.

"I delayed my wedding by a year, thanks to Mr. Wonderful here. I swear it's more than just the hours that keep Jared from the altar. It's the sordid details he listens to day after day. But CIIs aren't hard. All you have to do is hand the client tissues and tell her Tim Allen's right. Men *are* pigs.''

''I think I've got the first part down to a science.''

E.J. laughed. ''You'll get the hang of the second real quick. But your main purpose is to keep the clients from chasing Jared around the desk. I've been a regular at the CIIs ever since one client wanted more than tea and sympathy from Jared. He's just too damn sweet at these things.''

Alison understood that all too well. She'd been practically drooling over him during the meeting.

''I want to help my clients,'' Jared said in his defense. ''If I don't get the entire story of how the marriage failed, I can't get them everything they deserve under the divorce laws.''

''I think he just likes to hear the dirt,'' E.J. told Alison.

''Oh, yeah, I'm thrilled with—how did you put it, Alison?—what my half of the species does?'' Jared scoffed. He waved E.J. toward the door. ''Go back for more root canal, E.J. Make me a happy man.''

E.J. went out, laughing all the way.

''I'm sorry you sat in on the meeting with Mrs. Markson,'' he said when they were alone again. ''I just realized how unfair it was for you, to put you in what must have been an uncomfortable situation.''

''It's all part of the job,'' Alison assured him, smiling.

''We've got to pay you extra for that part of the job, that's for sure.''

''I won't say no.''

She gazed at him, again admiring his demeanor with his client…admiring the strong cleft to his chin and the beautiful blue of his eyes.…

She realized the silence between them had become

downright awkward. She stood. "I better go before *I* say something stupid this time."

Jared grinned slowly just as she recognized how revealing her words were. She blushed furiously, her face growing so hot so fast she was sure an egg would fry on it.

"I've said it, anyway," she admitted in a lame attempt at nonchalance, then rushed out of his office.

Alison managed to avoid Jared for what was left of the afternoon.

But she couldn't avoid her thoughts. Or her feelings.

JARED DRAGGED OUT his attributes list from his desk drawer at home. Although he'd kept the list in the back of his mind—had kept the thing for years—he hadn't actually looked at it in ages. But this whole business with Alison somehow had him thinking seriously about how much she did or didn't match up.

He stared at the slightly yellowed pages. Half the list looked more like a young man's arrogance than anything serious. Why had he wanted some of these things back when he was twenty? Youth. But he marked off Yes and No blocks on the right-hand side of the page to fill out as best he could what he knew or had observed about Alison.

IDEAL-MATE ATTRIBUTES
by Jared Holiday

I. Physical Beauty

    A. Dark hair, straight, preferably sophisticated style

    B. Doelike brown eyes

    C. Exotic features, delicate

D. Creamy skin, absolutely unblemished
E. Large breasts
F. Small waist
G. Long, slender legs
H. Petite frame, but negotiable as long as it looks good
I. Two years younger than husband (me)

Jared frowned. *A* through *E* were all no's. Her waist seemed normal, but she was a tall woman so it wasn't small. Her legs he couldn't really tell, not having seen the entire length of them. But he had hopes. *H* and *I* were a bust, too.

Hell, he thought.

II. Intelligence

A. MBA, at least
B. Attended Ivy League school
C. Have had at least one scholarship for grade-point average
D. Shrewd in personal finances
E. Can assess people and situations quickly

He had no clue on any of these, Jared admitted. She did seem to be able to do *E*, but he couldn't tell yet, either.

III. Personal Background

A. Personal wealth preferable, enough to live comfortably
B. Parents, relatives have personal wealth/no bums
C. Family name of some social standing

D. Race unimportant, but prefer Asian

Where the heck had *D* come from? Jared shook his head. OK, so he'd had a thing for Jenny Lee during his junior year of college. He thought Alison might be Irish, but the premise of *D* still stood. Race was unimportant for him.

"A 'yes!'" he exclaimed, and marked it off happily. Damn, at least she had one so far.

IV. Career

A. Well along her corporate ladder
B. Has a commitment to her job
C. Totally understands husband's needs with his job
D. Does not plan to interrupt career for family

"Oh, boy," Jared muttered. Alison wasn't even a no here; she was positively off the charts in the other direction.

V. Social Abilities

A. Adapts to any situation
B. Can talk with anybody about anything, knowledgeably
C. Thrives on social situations
D. Loves to entertain; last-minute guests are never a problem
E. Understands the importance of entertaining for husband's career
F. Will further her husband's cause in any way she can

G. Is active in at least two community organizations

Another clueless section, Jared acknowledged. He had a feeling this one would be a mixed bag when he finally found all the answers.

VI. Personal Likes and Dislikes

A. Takes great care of her person; always looks perfect day and night
B. Is a tigress in bed
C. Defers to husband's opinions, career and needs above her own
D. Wants two children and will be very giving mother to them
E. Likes nouvelle cuisine—cooks like a pro
F. Likes plays
G. Likes symphonies
H. Likes foreign films over domestic
I. Dresses in designer clothes, European flair
J. Likes jazz over other types of music
K. Generally very upscale in her total outlook
L. Calm nature; prefers smoothing matters over to fighting

Jared hoped *B* was a yes, a *big* yes. She wasn't close to *I*, and he had no clue about the others.

VII. Most Important

A. Love is not a requisite for her for marriage
B. She sees the value of good companionship and sharing similar interests with her husband
C. Although not a proponent of open marriage

> for herself, she will turn the occasional blind
> eye to her husband's outside needs

Jared had a feeling Alison and Most Important needed work, too.

> NOTE: Candidates must reach 90% of attributes for
> serious consideration.

Jared made a face. Just the few he could already check off about Alison showed she had a long way to go before she made the ninety-percent mark. Maybe he ought to change that to seventy-five percent. Maybe twenty-five percent would be more like it.

Jared cursed under his breath and put the list away.

Chapter Four

The King of Prussia Mall was huge.

Alison parked her car and got out. She glanced over at the mall, three football fields away, and told herself the exercise was good for her.

She made a face. Maybe she could find a tram car to bring her back.

"Hell," she muttered and began the trek to the mall entrance. Walking *was* good for one's health. It had better be.

She needed good health for a change. Her heart flutters and buzzing ears were almost chronic, even when she wasn't around Jared. And she thought about him continually. Like now. The FBI courses on psychology covered obsessiveness in detail. She was starting to fit that obsessiveness like a glove.

"Get him out of your mind," she said, muttering to herself again.

A couple and their two children veered away from her as they passed, clearly unsure of her sanity.

Alison grinned wryly. At this rate, she'd be on a bureau Wanted poster in every police station in the country.

Inside, the mall seemed even more huge—and upscale, with lots of little specialty shops. She wandered

along, observing the people shopping on a Thursday
night. Most were as upscale as the mall itself. At Nordstrom's, she browsed through the clothing department
and bought herself two suits, one blue and one black,
both with a salesclerk's help just to be assured of the
colors. The suits cost more than she'd earn this week at
Davis, Hansen and Davis.

Good thing she did have other financial resources, Alison thought. She needed them. On the other hand, she
didn't need the suits.

So why was she buying something that would help
her fit in better with Jared's life-style? The question was
better left unanswered, she decided.

Out of curiosity, she stopped at the home-furnishings
department. The prices on the rugs and furniture would
have eaten her FBI paycheck in a heartbeat. She shuddered and dropped the four-figure price tag attached to
a five-by-six carpet from Armenia. She couldn't see how
anyone could afford this *without* turning to a life of
crime. Still, this was a department store where one paid
top price for top quality....

"Thinking of buying?"

She jumped at the sudden voice behind her and
whirled around, not surprised to find Jared gazing at her.
She'd know that voice fifty years from now. A hundred.
He wore a chambray shirt and jeans, and looked even
more sexy than he did in his suits. Her heart pounded
and her ears rang. Yep, the chronic body noises were in
full force. Worse, her breast tingled with the memory of
his accidental touch.

"Hi," he said.

Alison drew in a deep breath. "Hi."

He smiled slowly, little laugh lines crinkling around
his eyes and kissable mouth. She'd never known a man's

lips could look that good, firm yet curving. He was innocent, boyish, tonight. Alison's heart melted. Her brain went out to lunch, but her hormones were in-house and raging.

"So are you thinking of buying?" he asked again.

"Oh. No," she replied, shaking her head. Good, she could still control movement. "Just browsing."

"Do you have a decorating job coming up?" he asked.

A decorating job…? Oh, yes, Alison thought, remembering the things she'd used to give her a background. Decorating had seemed safe enough. Lots of women dabbled in decorating, so it wasn't unusual and normally didn't prompt curious questions. Better still, it was hard to trace.

"Decorating's more of a hobby for me right now," she said. "It's a tough career to break into."

"I see."

She wondered what he saw, then decided not to worry about it. Tomorrow was her last day on the job.

"It's a great rug," he said. "Karaban is one of the best carpet companies in the business."

Karaban could have been a moratorium on carrots for all she knew about rugs, she thought in amusement. Aloud, she said, "Oh, absolutely. They're the best."

"So what did you buy?" he asked, pointing to the bag.

She glanced at the bag she held by its waxed-hemp handles. "Oh, a couple of…nice things. I haven't been shopping in a long time but it's…" What would be special enough to deserve a Nordstrom's buying spree? Especially on her temp salary? Only a divorce or a birthday came to mind. What the heck, she thought. "It's my birthday."

"Your birthday!" he exclaimed. "Congratulations!"

"Thank you," Alison said, feeling a bit of a fraud. She *was* a fraud. "Well, it was nice to see you, Jared."

"Oh, no. We've got to do something special for your birthday," he said, taking her arm.

"No, really," she began.

"Nonsense. There's a great food court downstairs. I'll treat you to a *latte* and a muffin with a birthday candle in it. Or is this a non-muffin-eating day?"

"It is, but really, Jared. You don't need to do this."

He ignored her, sweeping her along with him. She didn't know how to gracefully extricate herself, not since she'd created this birthday nonsense with her own big mouth.

"Thank you," she said humbly, while vowing to get her *latte* and get out as fast as she could.

Fortunately, the coffee shop had no birthday candles, so she passed up the muffin. Although she didn't normally drink coffee, she ordered a nonalcoholic Irish coffee decaf out of politeness. Her first sip surprised her.

"This is good!"

Jared grinned just before wiping the whipped cream of his hazelnut-and-vanilla *latte* from his mouth. *Too bad*, Alison thought. She would have loved to have kissed the cream off....

Good grief! Where had *that* come from?

"Happy Birthday, Alison."

"Thank you," she murmured again, then took a second sip of her coffee to clear away the self-disgust she suddenly felt.

"So what did you buy to treat yourself?" he asked.

"Oh, nothing special."

"Nothing special? Tsk, Alison. Everything is special

in Nordstrom's. Come on, you had to get something good.''

Hells bells, Alison thought. "I just got a couple of suits for the fall.''

"Suits? You?"

She lifted the bag onto her lap and opened it, then held up the jacket of one. "See? Just a simple suit.''

He chuckled. "It's blue.''

Alison's stomach clenched. Maybe she didn't have the color quite right or something. "Why? Is there something wrong with blue?''

"No. I just never thought of you as a blue-suit lady. In fact, I thought the opposite.''

"Well, I like a suit once a decade,'' she said, grinning at him. "Just to change things.''

"I can't wait to see you in it. What else did you buy for your birthday?''

She cleared her throat. "How's the black-suit lady sound?''

"Like a funeral director.'' He paused. "You didn't.''

She held out the jacket. "I am Have Black Suit, Will Travel.''

Jared burst into laughter. "I can't wait to see you in that one, too. You'll make one hell of a funeral director.''

"Dare to be different,'' she told him, smiling at his amusement.

"Those aren't birthday presents,'' he said. "Those are going-into-a-nunnery outfits. You're not going into a nunnery, are you?''

"Not me!'' But she laughed. The bureau had moments when it reminded her of a nunnery. "I don't know. The suits appealed because they were different, I suppose.''

"Drink your *latte* before you surprise me more," he said.

"All right."

As they both sipped their coffees, they chatted. Not about anything to require a past or future for herself. A good thing, Alison admitted. But their conversation made her feel comfortable and good about herself somehow—birthday fibs notwithstanding.

She also felt desirable, a condition that often passed her by with her lack of permanence. And she felt a little daring for being in the presence of a man who had touched her intimately, although accidentally. And she felt brave, too, just for talking with him without blushing and stammering. Bureau discipline had its good points every so often.

After their coffee, Jared strolled with her though the mall. They stopped at a bookstore to buy a book written by a cousin of his, the reason he was at the mall this night. According to Jared, he was under strict instruction to actually *buy* copies so his cousin, Michael Holiday, received full royalty and sales credit with his publisher. Alison gathered it had something to do with good retail-store sales ensuring Jared's cousin would continue to have a book career. She didn't know about how publishing worked, so she wasn't sure she had the process right.

Alison didn't recognize his cousin's name, since she moved around too much to regularly read a newspaper or this Michael's syndicated column. But the book title and its purpose appalled her.

"Man Can Live By Bread Alone?" she questioned, frowning at the cover, which depicted Jared's cousin and two bimbos in spandex. "What is this? A how-to-succeed-in-bachelorhood-without-trying guide?"

Jared chuckled. "Don't be so outraged. Michael's received the ultimate revenge. He just married a widow with six children, so I think the book's a moot point now."

"The poor woman," Alison lamented, as they waited in line to pay for the tome.

"Michael's wife, Janice, is an interesting woman, hardly long-suffering."

"She'd have to be to change a guy like that. What is he? A misogynist?"

Jared smiled slightly. "I suppose he was, a bit. My other cousin, Peter, recently married, too. Mary Ellen, his wife, is...unique in her way."

"Does he have a problem with women, too?" Alison asked, wondering about his family. "Don't tell me he wrote *The Joy of Bachelorhood in Five Easy Steps*."

"No. Peter's a research scientist."

"What was he researching? How to kill love in five easy lessons?"

"Actually, I think so."

She gaped at him. "You're kidding!"

Jared paid for the book. "No. At one time, he had some crazy notion that love was a chemical imbalance and made you crazy. I don't remember exactly. But he swore it could be controlled."

"But you can't control love," Alison said.

"No," Jared replied, gazing straight at her. "You can't."

Alison felt the very air between them charge with emotion. Her heart beat crazily; her ears rang with the bells of a thousand churches. Kaleidoscopes spun in her eyes. She couldn't pull her gaze from his.

"Excuse me, but I'd like to buy a book."

The next customer in line stepped between them, finally breaking the spell.

"Sorry," Alison said, the same moment Jared did.

They moved away from the counter. Neither of them said a word about cousins or love—or anything else—for a few minutes.

"Do you have any family here to celebrate your birthday with?" Jared asked finally.

Alison wished they were back talking cousins and love. Those subjects were less fraught with danger than her "birthday."

"No...I don't have family, actually." The less of "family" meant less questions for her to deal with.

"No family!" He stopped and gazed at her, sympathy clear in his expression. "Alison."

She smiled, touched by his concern. Lord, but it would be easy to eat this man up, even on a fast day. "I'm perfectly fine with it, Jared. Anyway, family can be a pain in the tush, or really mess you up forever at the worst. Believe me, there're many times when I'm glad to be independent."

Alison silently asked forgiveness of her mother and brother, who had provided her first with a home, and second, a loving family life.

He chuckled and began walking again. "Good point. My own parents have a love-hate relationship. They fight about everything, yet they won't divorce. They say it's a black mark in their social set. I think they just won't divorce, even though they make everyone around them miserable. As a kid, I felt caught in the middle. As an adult, I've been able to distance myself. Hell, I wish they'd come to me now as clients. I know they'd both be happier."

"Jared," Alison said, her sympathies rising to the surface. "You must have felt so alone as a child."

He grinned wryly at her. "Actually, I often wished they would get a divorce, so they could each be happy."

"Maybe that's why you're a divorce lawyer," she said. "You're trying to fix your parents' lives."

"Probably." He laughed, clearly enjoying the thought.

Alison relaxed, their conversation putting her at ease after the incident in the bookstore. If she didn't know better, she would have sworn she'd been in love.

Now that was an absolutely ludicrous notion.

Her back ached and her feet hurt from all the shopping and walking. Probably she was hallucinating from the pain. Shoppers delusion would go a long way to explaining that crazy moment in the bookstore with Jared.

She glanced at a clock in a jewelry store display window and groaned.

"Problem?" Jared asked.

Yes, you, she thought. Aloud, she said, "It's getting late and I should be going, but I was thinking of the expedition I'll have to make back to my car. I swear I parked a full mile away."

"This is the second-biggest mall in the Northeast," Jared said, chuckling. "Which means it's got the second-biggest parking lot. I used the valet service, so why don't we get my car and I'll drive you to yours? I'm ready to go, too."

Alison gaped. "This mall has valet service?"

"Lovely thought, isn't it? Too bad you missed it."

"Thanks for rubbing it in."

"You're welcome."

She knew she ought to part company with him now, but she couldn't resist the ride.

Sure enough, the damn mall did have valet service and she had missed it. She stood next to Jared at another mall entrance and watched the valet park Jared's BMW in front of them. Money exchanged hands, and that was that. So simple, she thought. So practical. So wonderful. Where the heck had her brain been?

She slid into the Beamer's passenger seat and sighed with pleasure. The buttery leather seats felt extra buttery at the thought of *not* walking to her car. Her tiredness had been washed away at the touch of luxury.

After Jared got behind the wheel, she said, "Thank you."

Jared chuckled. "You're that far out, eh?"

"Lord, yes."

"Want to tell me where?"

"I'm by the entrance near Sears."

"That *is* far. OK."

The car positively purred as he drove it around to the other side of the mall. Alison sat back and closed her eyes, savoring the ride and the spontaneous evening with Jared. Even the birthday fib faded. So the *latte* was ten months and six days early. She'd just remember it on her actual birthday, and his birthday "celebration" for her would count, wiping out today.

She would remember this "birthday" on every one of her real birthdays. And she'd wear the blue suit, or maybe the black, tomorrow. That seemed only appropriate.

"Don't fall asleep on me now," Jared warned. "You've got to tell me what row your car is in."

Alison opened her eyes and smiled at him. Then she glanced around the row signs hanging on parking-lot light posts. "Oh, boy..."

"What?"

"I don't remember exactly what row I'm in."

Jared burst into laughter.

"Look at this!" Alison exclaimed, waving at the sea of cars before them. "You tell me if you could remember where your car was in this."

"Why do you think I use the valet service?" Jared asked, his logic impeccable.

"I *will* find my car." Alison closed her eyes, remembering back. "I came in to the left of the entrance...one row...no, two rows over. And four sections back." She opened her eyes and pointed. "There! That row. Make a left onto it."

"If I make a right, I'll crash into the mall itself."

"Then you better make the left."

He made the appropriate left and drove up four sections. Alison's car sat just where she'd parked it.

"I *am* good," she murmured.

"That you are," Jared agreed.

Alison turned to him. She intended to thank him for his kindness earlier, and the ride to her car, but no words came out. Again that odd paralysis gripped her and she couldn't move.

Jared's gaze held steady on her face for the longest moment, as if he was memorizing her features. She would never forget his strong jawline and lambent blue eyes. His gaze lowered to her breasts, then rose again. Her whole body jolted in response.

"Tomorrow's your last day at the firm," he said.

She nodded.

"Does it matter now?"

It did. A lot. Alison found her voice. "No."

He leaned across the console and kissed her. She knew she should pull away, but his mouth started an instant fire inside her. Her blood heated and her body began to burn. Never had she had such an instantaneous reaction to a man's kiss. Her tongue met his without hesitation. Swirling…chasing…challenging…melding… His hand caressed her arm in long, slow strokes. His breath quickened as hers did when the kiss reached deeper. His fingers gripped her arm. Alison's head spun and her insides clamored with need.

At the moment when the kiss demanded all they had to give, they both pulled away. They stared at each other. Finally, Jared's hand dropped away.

"Thank you for the ride to my car," she said, wanting no misinterpretation. That her voice sounded normal gratified her.

"You're welcome." His voice sounded normal, too, to her bemusement. "Here, let me get your door—"

"No, no." She got out of the car before he could help her.

"I'll see you tomorrow," Jared said firmly.

She smiled. "Yes."

She meant it, too, and proved it by walking into Davis, Hansen and Davis five minutes early the next day. Since she had barely slept, she could have been a whole lot earlier. Mixed feelings were an understatement on this last day here—especially how she felt about Jared. Her lips still tingled from his kiss. What the rest of her body did was unspeakable.

After she settled at her desk, E.J. arrived.

"Alison, what do we have to pay you to take the secretary's job?" E.J. asked, deadly serious.

Temptations, Alison thought. "I can't, E.J. I'm just not interested in a permanent job now."

She already had one.

"I had a feeling you'd say that." E.J. frowned. "I have to admit that I've got a couple of other prospects.

I need to get Jared one of them pronto, but I wanted to offer it to you first. Are you sure you don't want the job?''

Alison resisted the urge to say no. What the heck was wrong with her? She didn't want to know, she decided. The answer could be scary. "I'm sure."

"I hate to lose a good person," E.J. said. "A little bird reminded me we want to archive some old files onto microfiche. I'd love for you to stay and do that. Please, please. It's temporary, but it'll give me time to change your mind. I'm not subtle."

Alison laughed. "E.J., there are plenty of good people looking for permanent work."

"You'd be surprised," E.J. said. "This microfilm job is right up your alley. Everything you want. Dull, boring, temporary. How about it?"

"Well…" Alison hesitated. She shouldn't, especially after last night. But she couldn't resist being around Jared just a little longer. If her FBI job ended before the microfiche task was finished, the temp agency could bring in a replacement. "All right."

"Hooray! I'll go call the temp service."

Alison nearly called E.J. back as common sense surfaced. Nearly.

Several hours later, after she returned from a break, a small, gaily decorated bag sat on her desk. No one was around.

"Oh, no," she muttered, her face flushing as she recognized what it was.

A birthday present.

She opened the bag, pushed aside the canary yellow tissue paper and peeked inside.

He'd given her a book. *Eating for your health.*

Alison laughed. She couldn't help it. The gift was

perfect, an inexpensive inside joke. He had figured out exactly the right thing that fit their personal and business relationship, one that couldn't be given back without looking small, mean and petty.

She opened the book. In the flyleaf, he'd written,

Alison, consider this a standing dinner invitation from me. In perpetuity. And maybe we could eat cake more than every other day? Jared.

"I thought you might like it."

Alison glanced up to find Jared standing in his office doorway.

"You shouldn't have. You *really* shouldn't have."

"I wanted to."

"Thank you," she said, feeling guilty as hell.

She bet her nose had grown three inches already.

JARED SMILED TO HIMSELF as he strode down the back hallways of Davis, Hansen and Davis Monday afternoon.

Alison was still here.

He had sensed she wouldn't take a permanent job with the firm, even though E.J. had been determined to ask her. One only had to hear her speak on the subject to know she was serious about continuing her temp work. So he'd talked to E.J. after court on Friday about the microfilming. E.J. had rocketed skyward with enthusiasm and had managed to convince Robert to begin the process. That Alison had agreed to stay on surprised and pleased Jared no end. He didn't want to read too much into it—nor too little.

Same with the kiss.

That had been one sweet kiss with a punch that had driven him through the roof. He had wanted to ask her out over the weekend, but knew he would scare her away if he tried. Not this early. That he had gotten away with the kiss—even under the guise of a birthday gesture—was enough for now. It had to be.

He heard Alison's radio before he turned into the file-room doorway. Four rows of huge, back-to-back, floor-to-ceiling file shelves ran down the length of a room the size of a small auditorium. "Miles of files" everyone called the room. It would take years to microfilm them all. Exactly his plan, Jared thought with satisfaction.

Alison sat at a desk. She fiddled with the microfilm viewer and cursed like a stevedore.

"I came to see how you were doing," Jared said. "But I think I just found out."

Alison sat back in her chair and looked at him with a hunted expression. She flipped her gorgeous hair off one shoulder. Why had he ever had a hankering for brunettes? Strawberry blonde was the most spectacular color.

She snorted in disgust. "E.J. showed me how to work this thing, but if it doesn't cooperate soon, I'm going to take it out and shoot it!"

Jared grinned. "Sure you can hit the side of a barn?" She didn't look it.

"I can hit a fly at twenty paces." She sounded deadly serious.

He wondered if she really were. He hoped not. Alison with a lethal weapon was a frightening notion.

"Here, let me see if I can help."

After all, he'd gotten her into this. He ought to try and get her out. He came around the desk and bent down, bringing himself into close proximity with her. Perfume and woman swirled through his senses. His mouth could taste hers all over again. His body could feel her breasts just brushing his chest all over again, too.

Damn, Jared thought, swallowing. He was ready to do a lot more than kiss her this time.

He noticed a red light blinking on the machine and read its small legend. "Here. There's a stop still on."

He flipped a switch and the machine began again, this time the light blinking green.

"What did you do?" Alison asked.

"I turned off the Stop switch. See? The light's green now."

"Oh." She brightened. "Oh! Great! Thanks."

"You're welcome."

He stood before he could attack her, not the very best thing to do when one wanted to score Brownie points as a gentleman. "E.J.'s interviewing permanent replacements for Elise for me...."

He paused, hoping she'd say, "Don't bother." She didn't.

"Did E.J. talk to you about splitting time between this and my needs until we hire someone?" he continued.

"Yes. This morning." Alison ran a couple of papers through the machine. "It works!"

"You're welcome again. Now about my stuff—"

"Just tell me what you need, and I'll take care of it."

She had no idea how tempting that offer sounded. How he wished she meant it the way he wanted her to.

As he told her what he needed with work, his brain assessed what he knew and didn't know about her. Damn little to the first, and barely anything to the second. She had no family; that was obvious from her birthday spree. Nordstrom's was not cheap. He had found out from E.J. what the agency paid Alison. The amount was so low Jared could not understand how she supported herself, let alone was able to afford one splurge at K mart.

All his sympathies had arisen that night at the mall. He had wanted to sweep her off her feet, take her to the best restaurant in the city, shower her with gowns and make it a birthday for her to remember always.

Instead, etiquette had forced him to offer a book and an Irish Creme coffee. He supposed it went with his now-subtle plan to get closer to her.

"Jared, there's something I want to talk with you about," Alison began.

Her tone sounded firm, triggering a warning in his brain. Warily, he said, "OK."

She glanced around the empty miles-of-files room, then said, "That kiss the other night...while I appreciated it—it won't happen again."

"It won't?" Jared echoed, his mind's eye seeing his subtle play go *poof.*

"No. It won't."

She looked at him sternly, reminding him of his third-grade teacher, Mrs. Swanson, who could glare the ice off the school roof in the dead of winter. Maybe it was the black suit Alison wore.

Alison continued, "I'm not interested in any kind of relationship, Jared. And I don't believe in office ones."

"I bet if I put you on the stand, I'd make a liar out of you," he said, before realizing how challenging that sounded.

"Jared—"

"No. No." He raised a hand, stopping her. "I have no business saying that. It was uncalled for, and I admit it."

"I hope you understand how I feel," she said.

He wanted to say a lot of things, understanding not

being one of them. But he forced himself to lie. "I do understand."

Good thing he wasn't a witness. He'd just perjured himself big-time. He'd now have to be more subtle than he'd thought with her.

Hell.

Alison relaxed in her chair. She smiled. "I'm glad we understand each other."

"Sure."

THREE DAYS LATER, he sat in his office, still muttering, "Sure."

He should have kissed her breathless the other day and then asked her if she'd thought one kiss was all there would ever be between them.

But no. He had to be *subtle*.

"Ass," he muttered to himself, having barely seen her since Monday afternoon. E.J. had hired a secretary for him, an efficient, older woman who was married and had three college-age children. She was fine, but he had no reason to see Alison, now relegated to the miles-of-files room full-time.

Now what?

Jared glanced around his office. The same old color schemes of blue and beige didn't register as he tried to think up a new plan for getting more intimate with Alison.

Then the colors hit him like a ton of bricks.

That was it! He sat up excitedly and stared around his office. He had had the same decor for years now—since he'd been given the office, really.

Alison was a decorator. A down-and-out one at the moment. If he got her decorating again, maybe she would be able to get a job in that field. Then all her valid arguments for nonrepeating kisses would become invalid. He dismissed her claim of not wanting a relationship. No man—or woman—was an island.

He should have thought of this before. It was perfect. He buzzed E.J. and asked her to send Alison to him.

She walked into his office five minutes later, a vision of loveliness wearing a brown skirt and a melon silk blouse. "E.J. said you wanted to see me."

"Yes, I did," he replied expansively. He gestured at his office. "Look around this room. What do you see?"

She looked around. "An office?"

"An *old* office. Does this office give off warm vibrations? No. Does it help my clients relax and express their pain more comfortably? No. Does it make them feel secure? No. Does it help them find a new life? No."

"That's a lot to ask of an office," Alison said.

"It is. But it has to be done. I want you to redecorate my office."

"Me?" she squeaked, her eyes widening with shock.

"Sure. You were a decorator—"

"I *worked* for one—"

"Same thing."

"No, it's not."

"This is a great opportunity for you to resharpen your skills," he said.

"I can't!" she protested.

"I'm not taking 'no' for an answer," Jared countered. And he didn't.

Chapter Five

Alison touched her nose, surprised to find it *hadn't* grown from yet another fib come to life.

Decorating his office!

She had spent twenty minutes in his office, trying to talk him out of looming disaster. She had pleaded and refused outright to do the job. He absolutely insisted she redo his office. Sir Walter Scott's sentiment about tangled webs had nothing on her.

For a week now she'd been walking around, trying to come up with a way to get out of it. Barring leaving. That was her last resort. Her last resort was right around the corner.

Alison flipped through a woman's magazine while she sat out on a picnic bench and ate her lunch. The bucolic atmosphere provided here on the grounds of the Davis, Hansen and Davis building ought to distract her—the beautiful, late-summer blue sky with its puffy clouds; the turning leaves on the trees; the green, green grasses and the opening mums; the cars buzzing by on Route 30....

They helped but not much.

"Great," she muttered. Maybe the magazine had an article on how a woman could kill a man with her bare hands. Now that would be *very* helpful. Surely there was one.

"I thought that was you out here."

Alison looked up from the magazine. Jared, naturally, walked toward her. No one else sneaked up on her quite the way he did. Love stories suggested a woman was aware of a man before he was even in the room. Not her, Alison thought. Her awareness never kicked in until after the fact. And then it went off like a hydrogen bomb. Maybe because it was on overload in his presence, her brain just shut everything down in between times.

Sure enough, her heart pounded and her body throbbed just from her looking at him. He gave a woman a lot to look at, especially with the way his trousers clung in the right places and his shirt fit his broad shoulders and narrow waist. The suspenders he wore only added to his image. "Styling," the kids called it. Jared could style.

"Hi," she said.

He sat down next to her on the bench, then poked at her paper bag. "I'm too late to take you to lunch. Is this a fruit day or regular?"

"Regular."

"Wow. And I missed it. So what did you have? Chocolate cake and a side of beef? Two blueberry-fed chickens and pizza with the works? Fettucini Alfredo?"

"A ham-and-cheese sandwich and chips." She focused in on his own menu. "Are you a Nero Wolfe fan?"

He chuckled. "The chickens gave me away, didn't they?"

She smiled. Her body calmed a little bit—but just a little bit. "I love those mysteries. I'm so glad Stout was prolific."

"And lived to be eighty-eight. I think they're great, too."

Alison was a voracious reader. Unfortunately, she had to give books away, not able to carry them all with her when she traveled for the job. She couldn't send every one home to her mother.

She and Jared talked books for a few minutes, finding mutual pleasure in several authors. Alison wasn't sure she truly liked knowing they had mutual pleasures. If they did in one area, they might in others. He was too tempting as it was.

"How's the new secretary?" she asked, curious and needing to change the subject.

"She's not you."

The words gave her far too much pleasure.

"But she's a good secretary," Jared admitted.

"Good," Alison said, trying to mean it.

Jared turned the open magazine toward him. "Hey! This is nice. Is this what you're thinking of doing to my office?"

Alison's mouth dropped open. She looked at the layout. A sofa and several comfortable-looking chairs were grouped in an intimate arrangement. Warm yellows and what looked like soft greens were the predominant color schemes. A painting of a waterfall and other touches enhanced the cozy atmosphere. Yet the furnishings had a professional look to them, one that could easily translate into an office decor.

She couldn't. She shouldn't.

"I was considering it as an option," she said, putting a finger against her nose to keep it from growing. One never knew.

"I really like it. Do you think, as a woman, you would

be comfortable in this? Comfortable enough to tell me, your divine lawyer, what I would need to know?''

Alison thought she'd spill her beans at a crowded MacDonald's restaurant if Jared were the questioner. ''Yes, I think so. But what about your male clients? Would they respond or would they be put off by an office like this?''

Jared frowned and stared at the picture. ''The throw pillows might put off a guy. I could hide them in a closet when I have a male client come in. I don't have a lot of men clients, though.''

''I'm not surprised,'' Alison murmured.

''Now what's that supposed to mean?''

She swallowed. She didn't want to think what she meant by her remark, let alone tell *him*. ''Well...I think you relate better to women. You've got a sympathetic manner they respond to.''

''I see,'' he said, relaxing. ''Do you respond to it?''

Alison straightened, a sudden chasm opening in front of her. One misstep and she'd be over the edge. ''I thought we agreed not to discuss anything personal between us.''

''No. We agreed not to *do* anything personal,'' he countered, grinning at her. ''We never agreed to not discuss anything. So do you respond to my sympathetic nature?''

''Now wait a minute,'' she began, determined to argue about the rules of their ''relationship.''

''Jared!''

She turned with Jared at the sound of his name. Alison stifled a groan when she saw the caller was Robert Davis. He strode toward them like a man on a mission.

''Afternoon, Robert,'' Jared said.

"What are you doing out here?" Robert asked, looking intently at both of them.

"Enjoying the weather."

Robert frowned. "I don't know that it looks good, Jared."

"The weather looks great, Robert."

"No. I mean..." Robert waved a hand at the two of them. "This."

To Alison's amazement, Jared chuckled. "*This* looks fine. Join us and we'll look so confident of our abilities as attorneys that we can take a few minutes to smell the roses, as the saying goes. Besides, we'll be inside soon enough when winter comes. Sit down, Robert, and look confident. I wanted to talk with you about a new project."

Robert glanced at Alison. For once his gaze wasn't vitriolic. "Another time. I have a client arriving in a few minutes." He refocused on Alison. "You're doing other work for us now, aren't you?"

"I'm microfilming the file room," Alison replied, smiling.

Robert made a face. "I suppose it's necessary."

"Absolutely, it's necessary," Jared said. "Have you been in there lately? There're files that go back to your grandfather's time."

"Really?" Robert's eyebrows shot up. "I wasn't aware of that."

Alison bet there were tons of things this guy wasn't aware of.

"You've got to lose a secretary occasionally. It's an eye-opener, believe me."

Alison knew Jared was talking about more than finding a file. She resisted the urge to kick him under the table. She'd have to kick him sideways, which would only be a glancing blow, not worth the effort.

Robert actually smiled. "I think I'll pass."

After the head of the firm was headed back into the building, Jared turned to her. "He intimidates you."

"No," Alison said. "I have nothing to say to him, that's all."

"Robert is a…difficult man, as you've already gathered. His heart's in the right place, but his methods need a crash course at diplomacy school."

Alison shrugged. "It doesn't matter to me how an employer behaves. I'm not beholden to one particular job, so I'm not bothered by a *difficult*—your word—boss."

"Well, you'll be at this job for a while," Jared said. "Now, back to where we were when Robert interrupted us—"

"Sorry, but my lunch hour is over." Alison belatedly glanced at her watch. *Close enough,* she thought. "Back to work for me."

"But the decorating job—"

"I know what you want now." Alison stood and gathered her bag of trash and the magazine. "I still think you ought to hire a real decorator."

"I thought I had."

Alison clamped her lips shut. She'd walked into this mess and now couldn't walk out without exposing her real job, something that was forbidden by the bureau. She had to be a true mole, to find out how potential "clients" would live in the area. Besides, no one would be comfortable discovering that "ordinary" people weren't ordinary. Citizens would feel as if they were in a totalitarian country, no matter how benign the reason. The uproar would be tremendous.

If it got out.

It wouldn't from her. "So how do you want to pay for this? Cash or credit card?" she asked, then laughed at his surprised expression.

"Cash, I guess. Do you want a deposit?"

"I'll let you know."

That night, she walked through the doors of an independent furniture store and asked to see the manager. She was shown into an office where a woman sat behind a desk.

"Can I help you?" the woman asked.

"I hope so." Alison laid the magazine open on the desk, the picture Jared liked facing up. She pointed to it. "Can you get this *exactly*? All the manufacturers are listed on the page turned down in the back."

The woman raised a perfectly groomed eyebrow, then studied the picture. She flipped the magazine pages until she reached the list, which she studied for a few moments. "Yes, provided the manufacturers have these colors still in stock."

Oh, Lordy, Alison prayed. *Please have everything exact in stock or I'll be dead meat.* "Good. I want this room exactly as it's shown. Everything in the photo from the wall scones to the couch. How soon can you get it?"

"Depends. Some companies take a week, some as many as six to ship in-stock furnishings."

"Oh, I'll need the place papered in that wall covering. Can you recommend somebody?" *Hey,* she thought. If she was going to do this, she might as well go all the way.

"There are several paperhangers I can recommend."

"How much of a deposit will you require?" Alison asked.

"Five thousand."

Alison grinned. What the heck. It wasn't her money and it would serve Jared right. "Done. I'll bring you a check tomorrow."

The woman sat back and chuckled. "Gosh, that was one of the easiest sales I've ever made."

Alison laughed.

This was fun.

"WHAT THE HELL do you mean, I've got to clear out my desk this weekend?"

Jared gaped at Alison, who stood on the other side of the article under discussion. She looked positively gleeful.

"You want your office redone or not?"

"Redone."

"The decorator fairies are on strike, so that means you have to do it. Oh, and your file credenzas will have to be pulled out so the paperhangers can work on the walls."

Jared told himself the chaos was for a good cause. It had better be. "OK."

Alison walked around his office, inspecting it. "I'll have to take down the pictures and things so I'll need boxes for them. Can I donate the old stuff to a local shelter to help dress it up or do you have plans for these things?"

"No, no plans," Jared said, feeling overwhelmed.

"Good. I'll need a check made out to A and M Furnishings, for five thousand dollars."

"Five thousand dollars?"

"That's just the deposit."

"Deposit!" He got out his checkbook, muttering the entire time he wrote out the check. The things he did for…he wasn't sure exactly what he was doing it for, but his libido damn well better appreciate it.

"Someone will have to open the office on Saturday for the workers," Alison said.

"I guess that's me," Jared muttered.

"They assure me they'll only need a weekend to hang the paper. I'll need a check for them for three thousand."

"Three thousand?" Jared rose out of his seat in shock.

"That's their deposit, Jared. Blaine's Hanging Service." Alison eyed him sternly. "What did you expect? That I could wave a wand and your office would be redone in an instant, scot-free?"

"I was hoping for that," he admitted.

Alison sighed and shook her head. "Men."

Women, he thought. She was like a drill sergeant today, issuing orders and making demands. What had happened to the ditzy woman who had walked into the firm on Labor Day?

"Today's a fast day, right?" he said, remembering her lunch bag of yesterday.

"Yes. Why?"

"Just checking." She hadn't turned completely into Genghis Khan. The flower child still reigned somewhere. Jared pointed to the statuette on his desk. "One thing. Justice stays. I've had her since college."

"I will handle her myself with great reverence," Alison promised.

"Good." Jared grinned at her, feeling somewhat mollified.

"Now write the check," she commanded.

"I'm writing, I'm writing!"

This had better be worth it, he thought.

Saturday morning, he was positive his decorating scheme was *not* worth it. His office was a shambles of covered furniture piled in the middle of the room. Make-shift scaffolds stood in splendor along the walls. The yeasty odor of wallpaper paste permeated everywhere. Men in overalls slapped long strips of textured paper on the wall while a radio blared the latest in pop, rap and *nouveau* disco.

The only saving grace was Alison herself, who stood next to him and surveyed the workers. Her jeans clung to her legs and her short top just skimmed her waistband. Occasionally, he got a peek at creamy midriff—and some freckles. She wore her hair in a thick ponytail that just touched her nape. Her face glowed with personal satisfaction and her eyes sparkled with excitement.

Jared smiled. He'd known it was right to help put her back on track. The job might cost a bundle but it *was* worth it to see her happy. Maybe she would get a job in her field again—and he would be home free.

"Break time," someone said.

"They just started!" Jared yelped in astonishment.

"They're union," Alison said, shrugging.

"But this will never be done by Monday," he said.

"I'm sure it will be." She smiled. "You're paying them time and a half. Double for tomorrow."

"Double!" Jared cursed heartily. He glanced at his watch, then glanced up again. "Tomorrow! How are they getting in? And why do I already have a sneaking suspicion I know?"

"I told you about this," Alison said, shaking her head.

"You just said Saturday."

"No, I said 'weekend.'"

"No, Saturday." He waved a hand. "What does it matter and what time do I have to be here?"

"Ten. They have church."

He glanced at the long hair and beards of several workers. "This crew?"

"It's the best place for sinners to repent," Alison said. "You ought to go."

"I don't need to. I'm repenting already."

Alison just laughed.

Jared grabbed his notebook computer and headed for the outer office. He couldn't watch anymore. Grumbling his way through some files, he vented his frustration. Later this afternoon, he had to go to a barbecue at his cousin Michael's house. Fresh from his wedding, Michael had invited the family over. Jared didn't know if he'd get there now.

Alison, to his further frustration, sat at another desk, with her feet up on the desktop as she read a book. How could she be so calm? How could he wheedle his way closer?

About two o'clock, however, the men filed out of his office, tool bags and radio in hand.

"Quitting time," one of them said, grinning as they walked by.

Jared gaped while they filed past. He turned to Alison. "They're quitting now?"

"Sure. It's Saturday."

"But they've barely worked!"

"Nonsense. You'd be surprised how much pros can do in a few hours."

Jared saved his working file, then went into the office. Two walls were covered with drying paper. He gaped again, this time because she was right. Finally, he smiled. This crazy notion of his might actually work. Then he frowned. "The paper looks a little dark."

"It does?" Alison whipped around to stare at the

walls. "The paper's still wet. That's probably why. It should lighten when it's thoroughly dry."

"You should know." Jared smiled expansively, then not quite so expansively when he thought about the workmen leaving early. But they had done him a favor.

Suddenly, he had a brainstorm.

"What are you doing the rest of the day?" he asked.

"Well…" she began.

"Good. You're free. Since you've turned my office upside down, you can come with me to a barbecue in Jersey."

"Oh, no. I couldn't."

"Oh, yes, you can. You owe me."

"Jared—"

"Don't bother to argue. I'll win again, anyway."

"Look at where that got you," she responded, waving her hand around his disaster of an office.

"Good point, but I'm willing to try again."

She did argue against going with him, but he held firm until she finally collapsed. "All right. I'll go."

"Good."

She glared at him. "You are—"

"A very good lawyer?" he suggested.

"A pain in the tush," she countered.

He chuckled. At least they were talking anatomy.

He drove them both over to Michael's house, leaving her car in the office parking lot. Since she didn't know the way and evidently didn't know the area well, his driving them seemed easier. Plus he had her close to him, something he liked a lot.

But her ignorance of local geography sent an alarm bell off inside him. He knew she temped. He knew she was from Chicago originally. He knew she had no family. But he hadn't thought her *that* new to the area.

He forgot the disturbing thoughts when they arrived at Michael's. Amy, Michael's stepdaughter, practically flew at them in her excitement.

"Hi, Uncle Jared," she chirped, already incorporating him and his cousins into her newly extended family. "My daddy's cooking and my mommy's yelling at him. Who's that lady?"

"This is Ms. Palmer," Jared told Amy. "She works at my office."

"Hi," Amy called across the seat to Alison. "Do you like hamburgers and hot dogs?"

"I do," she replied, smiling. "And my name is Alison." She got out of the car before Jared could help her.

Amy went around to her. "I have a girl in my class named Alison, but she has brown hair. I like yours."

"Thank you. I do, too."

Jared smiled at the picture Alison made with Amy. He could easily imagine a miniature Alison, full of innocence and joy, blurting out anything that came to mind. Maybe little Alison would have his eyes....

Where the hell had that come from?

Jared mentally shook himself. It was one thing to want Alison in his bed. It was quite another to want children. Maybe he'd been having some thoughts about a future. Maybe he was in a tailspin about Alison—God knows, she could spin his tail anytime. But that didn't mean future and tailspin went together.

Amy chattered away as she walked between them around the house to the backyard. Alison smiled a little too sweetly at him over the child's head.

"Is this a family party?" she asked, when Amy took a breath.

"Oh, yes," Amy said happily. "Uncle Peter and Aunt

Mary Ellen are here already. And Uncle Raymond's here, too. But he didn't bring a lady with him.''

"Jared!" Alison muttered angrily.

"It's perfectly fine," Jared replied confidently. "You won't even know it's anything but a meal."

In the backyard, Michael slaved over the barbecue pit. Flowers bloomed everywhere, many in early autumn colors. Jared didn't know their names, but Michael and Janice, avid gardeners, did.

Janice, Michael's wife, actually lived behind Michael's house here. The two had met when Michael moved in earlier in the year. They weren't sure which house they would keep, although Michael, a writer, used his old office, while he lived with Janice and the kids in her own house. He half kidded that they would keep his house as a refuge from the children.

Janice's triplets, Cat, Chris and C.J., played soccer with Raymond in the very back of the yard. Janice's older son, David, helped Michael at the barbecue, while her eldest daughter, Heather, sat with some of her friends. The extra kids gratified Jared. Alison wasn't the only outsider today.

Jared shook hands with the kids and with Peter and Michael. He waved to Raymond and kissed the two wives on the cheek, introducing Alison all around as he did.

Janice welcomed Alison with a genuine smile. "You are a brave soul for coming to our madhouse."

"It's nice of you to have an unexpected guest," Alison said.

"Pooh!" Mary Ellen exclaimed. "Janice isn't fazed by another mouth to feed. What's one more with her crowd?"

"Our crowd!" Michael corrected, from the smoking grill. He nudged David, who grinned at him.

"Just don't burn the hamburgers," Janice warned her husband. "But don't forget to burn my hot dog or you can sleep alone tonight!"

"Just promise to throw the cat out of our bedroom, and it's yours. The damn thing keeps sniffing my face at three in the morning."

"Michael loves you, Michael," Janice said, grinning at her husband.

"Yeah, Daddy. Michael the cat loves you," Amy repeated, laughing.

The human Michael made a face at her, sending her into a fit of giggles.

"I'll make sure he gets it right, Mom," David promised.

"Thanks, golf boy," Michael groused. "Next time *you* carry the bags. Maybe I'll win for once."

David just laughed at his stepfather.

Alison turned to Jared and whispered, "That's the one with the book about permanent bachelorhood?"

Jared chuckled. "In the flesh."

"He seems so normal."

"He married a woman with six children. You tell me."

"Good point."

They settled into lawn chairs next to Mary Ellen and Peter. Mary Ellen smiled at her and Jared. "Well, this is an interesting turn of events. *Very* interesting. I thought you were a workaholic, Jared, and had no time for women. Except as clients."

"I was at the office until I came here. Right, Alison?"

"Right," Alison said warily. "And I only work with Jared."

Jared glanced at her porcelain skin and sassy ponytail. He wanted to do a whole lot more than work with Alison.

"Hmm…" Mary Ellen mused. "Working overtime. Peter, remember when we worked overtime at your lab?"

"Chemistry," Peter said, patting her knee. "It's a beautiful thing."

"I'm just his decorator," Alison explained. "He's redoing his office."

"Didn't you have your office decorated already?" Peter asked.

Alison snapped her head around to glare at Jared.

"When I moved into the office years ago, yes, I had it redone," Jared replied, giving his cousin the evil eye.

"Are you sure?" Peter asked, totally innocent.

Mary Ellen kicked him in the shin. "Excuse my husband. He wouldn't remember his name if people didn't say it to him all the time."

"I'm not *that* bad," Peter retorted. "And you hurt me."

"I'll kiss it later."

"Promise?" Peter asked eagerly. "All the way up my leg?"

"What a baby you are," his wife chided, grinning at him.

Jared glanced at Alison. Her face was rosy, and she was looking studiously at the soccer game. He knew—*knew*—that she was having the same thoughts he was—all primitive and all for each other. Suddenly, he had that familiar heart-pounding, blood-beating reaction to just being in her presence. Everything seemed to fade until only he and she were left in sharp, clear relief.

Alison turned. Her gaze met his. It was as if he could

see every thought she had. Every emotion. She wanted him, yet feared losing herself forever. He wanted her stripped as naked as her soul was to him now. He wanted to meld with her, to taste every inch of her flesh, to capture her heart....

"Geez! Not you, too!"

Jared blinked, coming back to earth. Raymond stared at him in disgust, while Peter and Mary Ellen burst into laughter. Clearly, the soccer game had broken up in favor of dinner.

"I think this is the Year of the Rat, not the year of the marriage," Raymond said.

"I think it's the year of the bunny," Mary Ellen commented.

"Daddy! Can I have a bunny?" Amy shouted, having caught the end of the conversation.

"What bunny?" Michael shouted back from the grill.

"It's the Year of the Ox," Peter said.

"You need an ox, honey," Mary Ellen told Amy.

"Daddy, I want an ox." She turned to Mary Ellen. "What's an ox?"

"It's the year of the something," Raymond commented.

"I think you're mistaken about my relationship with your cousin," Alison began. "I'm only a temp at Jared's office."

"And his decorator," Peter added, he and his wife laughing all over again.

"Stop abusing the guest, please," Jared told his family. "Poor Alison will probably kick me from here to Kingdom Come for bringing her today."

Mary Ellen leaned forward and said to Alison, "We're not this bad. Honest. It's just that Jared makes such a nice target. So does Raymond."

"What's happening with this crowd?" Raymond asked, but didn't wait for an answer. "I tell you, it's not going to happen to me. I'm taking Michael's advice, even if he didn't. 'Women are like fine wine. Sample a lot but don't stick to any one bottle.'"

"Once you have the best, you don't need the rest," Michael's wife said, having heard her cousin-in-law's remarks. "Michael found the best, now leave him be, Raymond, or Mary Ellen and I will fix you up with a woman."

Raymond shuddered. "I'll be good. I promise."

"I thought so."

"Is it a faux pas to say this is a crazy family?" Alison asked.

Mary Ellen crowed with amusement. "I like this girl, Jared."

"Me, too," Jared agreed.

"Now, wait a minute..." Alison said, continuing to protest to Mary Ellen. Not about her being nice, but about her and Jared's relationship.

Jared sat back and listened to the conversation. This family gathering triggered an emotional memory. He felt a warmth and affection surrounding him that he hadn't in years. The good-natured teasing reminded him strongly of when he and his cousins had been boys around their grandmother's dinner table.

He glanced at Alison, who was now being whisked along by his cousins' wives to help set out dinner. She could bring back those great feelings even more.

Later that night, as he drove her to pick up her car, Jared pondered how to draw her closer to him. He had to be patient, but he also needed a new angle to invade her life.

"Thank you for taking me to your family outing,"

Alison said, when he parked next to her lone car at the lot.

"You're welcome. Did you have fun?"

She smiled reluctantly. "A bit. The kids are a lot of fun. So are the adults. But you really gave them the wrong impression about us."

"Did I?" He smiled. "They *are* a crazy family. Who knows where they get their notions?"

"It explains your cousins. I still can't believe Michael is the author of that chauvinistic book. He's positively docile. Certainly, he's domestic."

"He's in love with his wife and children." Jared envied Michael. Even the triplets were slowly coming around to their new father. And Peter's Mary Ellen radiated spontaneity.

Jared wondered if he put too much stock in his list of perfect-women attributes and not enough in letting his body find the right person. But that was the whole point of the list—to avoid having his gonads make a mistake.

"I better go," Alison said, opening the car door.

"Wait." He got out and came around to her side. After he opened the door wider, he said, "You've got to slow down, Alison, and let me be a gentleman."

He put out his hand to help her. She hesitated one telling second, then took it. Jared felt the shock of her touch all the way up his arm. Lightning couldn't have shaken him more. He pulled her up out of the seat and straight into his embrace.

The kiss was all pent-up hunger, and she met it fully. Her body pressed to his; her arms wound around his neck. Her mouth was cool fire.

Jared wanted more, yet was content with this taste of her. After all, she'd said it would never happen another time.

"So much for not doing this again," he said, when the kiss finally ended.

"*That* was the exact wrong thing to say," Alison said, pulling out of his embrace.

Jared gaped. "Alison—"

"Forget it." She unlocked her car door.

Everything that had been perfect a minute ago now unraveled faster than a sweater thread caught on a door splinter. "Allie. Honey—"

"I'm not Allie, and I'm no honey. Thank you for a lovely evening."

"Decorate my house!" he yelped, as she got in her car.

"No! Are you nuts?"

"No! It would be perfect." It was perfect. She'd be in his house and he could patch up the mistake he'd made tonight. Whatever the hell it was.

"Absolutely not."

She hadn't slammed the car door on him. She was listening. Jared began his argument. "You need the work—"

"Hah!" She slammed the door shut and started her car. Listening time was over.

"I won't take no for an answer," he told her through the closed window.

In response, she pulled out of the slot, burning rubber as her car squealed out of the parking lot.

"Good," Jared said, watching her go. "That's all settled."

Chapter Six

"I hear you're decorating Jared's house," E.J. said, as soon as she saw Alison on Monday morning.

"I'll kill him!" Alison exclaimed, marching toward his office.

"He's in court," E.J. said.

"Good. I'll save the county gas money for my arrest."

E.J. laughed.

Alison didn't. What a mess this had become. "I am not decorating his house, E.J."

"He seems to think you are," E.J. replied, grinning. "I think you ought to. Maybe he'll go home occasionally, instead of living at the office like he does."

"I'd love to hog-tie him there," Alison said in frustration.

"Oh, boy. Kinky stuff. Let me know how it goes, and I'll try it with my husband. We could use a lift in our love life right now."

"I don't have a love life," Alison said sternly.

E.J. just looked at her with *that* look.

"Honest!"

"What you say and what you want may be two different things,'' E.J. said. ''Go. Decorate his house. I like what you've already done with his office.''

Alison groaned and walked away. ''I've got to work, E.J. You pay me for that, remember?''

Back in the file room, Alison sat down in front of the microfilm machine. Creating a false life might be necessary, but it also created havoc, especially when people actually paid attention to what she said. This whole decorating business was out of hand. Way out of hand.

And his family's barbecue! She'd thought it would be a casual meal with friends, *not* an intimate family affair. She never would have gone if she'd known. The cousins had been charming, although Raymond needed work. The kids had been raucous, but courteous. Alison envied Jared his family, even an extended one. Her job rarely allowed her to get back home.

The wives had been informative during cleanup. Alison had learned more about Jared than she cared to—at least on a logical level. On an emotional one, she needed to hear about the grandmother's affair that had affected all the boys—or so Mary Ellen and Janice postulated. Alison also needed to know about his parent's loveless marriage. She now understood Jared much better, knowing his background.

And she melted all the more for him, even though angry with his stupid comment after he'd kissed her. Unfortunately, the stupidity was all on her end. *She* had needed to turn away, not kiss him as breathlessly as he kissed her. Why wouldn't he think she'd kiss him again and again after that? She would. She wanted to. Dammit!

She could get out of all this by disappearing. Running away solved nothing, however, and finishing a job was too ingrained in her. Besides, she disliked leaving people in the lurch.

Alison pursed her lips. OK, so she'd have to decorate his house. It might be more intimate than she preferred, but she could handle it. A couple of pictures and then turn it all over to the furniture store and the paperhangers.

No problem—as long as she kept her head. Was she an FBI agent or a mouse?

"Don't answer that," she muttered.

She marched into his office about four-thirty in the afternoon, armed with magazines she'd bought during her lunch hour.

"Hey! I thought my office was supposed to be finished," Jared said, waving to the still-discombobulated room. "Where's the rest of the furniture? And the wallpaper's different from the picture."

Alison stopped and stared at the walls. They weren't as bright as the photo had shown, the background color more dark cream, almost beige, rather than cream-white. *Great,* she thought. *Now what?* Still, relief might be spelled "wrong color." "Since you're not happy with the office decor, I probably shouldn't do your house."

"No, no." He waved his hand again. "It's still drying...."

"After three days?"

"Sure. Good thing I didn't have client appointments today. I'll use the conference room until this one's ready." He grinned, looking so good that Alison felt her insides turn to mush. "So you *will* do my house."

"Oh, ah…" *Get your brain together,* she told herself, then said aloud, "All right. I will."

Get it over with and get out. Besides what the hell could be left *to* decorate? With that in mind, she slapped magazines down on his desk.

"What's this?"

"Your new decor. I marked the pages. I don't know how many bathrooms or bedrooms you have, so I picked three bathrooms and four bedrooms. And a den-cum-home office, in case you have one of those. I assumed you do."

Jared stared at her. "But don't you have to see the house? Take measurements or something?"

"That's overrated," she said airily. "Just pick what you like and I'll get it."

Jared frowned, then looked at the various pages she'd marked. "I don't want country French or retro sixties, like these."

"You don't?" she squeaked, panic sweeping through her gut.

"No. I don't even think they go together in the same house."

"They don't?" She mentally shook herself. "I thought it would be...kicky."

"Well, I sort of like this." He pointed to one. "But not this exactly. And these two bathrooms won't work at all in my house."

"They won't?"

He shook his head. "No. They won't. You better come to the house tonight. How about right after work? I'll make dinner for us."

"Oh, no. I couldn't do that." God help her if she did.

"OK, then I'll come to your place and we can brainstorm."

Her place was a hotel room. *Trapped,* Alison thought, feeling like a mouse lured by a nice piece of aged Vermont cheddar. The lesser of two evils it was. "Dinner at your place will be fine. But just dinner."

"And a grand tour." His smile, however, reminded

her of more intimate encounters with him. Kissing encounters.

Somehow, Alison didn't throw herself in his arms. "And a grand tour."

The "wisdom" of her decision hit home the moment she entered his house. She felt very comfortable, a surprising reaction when she had expected nervousness. Panic, really. If anyone told her she was an FBI agent on a mission, she wouldn't believe them. She felt very much like a temporary secretary in the house of a sexy man.

He took her into his kitchen and sat her on a counter stool where she could watch him cook.

He was good, flipping vegetables sautéing in a pan just as the professional chefs did on television. He even wore a pristine, white chef's apron, the ties wrapped around his trim waist before meeting in a cute bow in front. Alison's brain conjured up the image of him in *just* the apron.

Lord, but E.J. was right, she decided. She was getting kinky.

"I thought you might like a paella variation I learned years ago," Jared said. "It's with more vegetables and less rice, almost like a ragout."

"You'll make some wife a great cook," Alison said, sipping the white wine he'd put in front of her earlier.

Jared grinned. "I hope so."

That remark was better left unexplored, so Alison looked around the kitchen. Its cabinets and wall coverings were bright, unnicked and generally a chef's dream. He cooked at an island equipped with an indoor grill. Gleaming copper pots and pans hung on a rack above his head. The other appliances were ultramodern and couldn't be older than a year or two at most. Same with the white cabinets trimmed in brown, the cheerful wall-paper and the country, hardwood floors.

"Jared, this room doesn't need a makeover," she said, glaring at him. "It's perfect. In fact, so is the foyer. The glimpses I got of your living room and dining room look like a house to kill for. Why would you change any of it?"

"I'm bored with it all," he said, splashing wine into the frying pan. The food ignited.

"Jared!" Alison exclaimed, startled by the sudden fire and appalled by his attitude.

He clamped a lid on the pan, snuffing the flaming alcohol. "I meant to do that. Would you like more wine?"

"No." She put her hand over the top of her glass when he would have poured her more. She was afraid she might go up in flames like the vegetables.

"You sure?" he asked, holding the light green bottle up. "It's a white chardonnay from a very good California winery."

"I'm sure," she said firmly. Feeling comfortable was one thing; getting drunk was damn dangerous. "Jared, is all this decorating business a ploy?"

"For who? For what?" he asked, looking innocent.

Alison realized the only answer she had was, "For me. For sex." Her ego must be the size of a watermelon. He might be attracted to her, but no man would spend tens of thousands of dollars in decorating office and home, just to lure a woman into his bed. Unless she was a supermodel.

Alison was no supermodel.

OK, so he made her feel that way sometimes, but she had to get a grip on reality.

"I'll make the salad," she volunteered, to keep herself from staring gooey eyed at him.

"I've got some escarole and Bibb, as well as tomatillos, peppers, cucumbers and carrots," he said. "They're in the fridge. You can shred the carrots in the processor."

"Whatever happened to good old salad in a bag?" she muttered under her breath while rummaging around in his refrigerator. Good thing she hadn't listed chef in her fake background. Jared would probably have her making beef Wellington and rumaki or something equally high cuisine and complicated.

Instead, she would make salad and get out of this new decorating job.

Dinner was terrific. She wished she didn't know he could cook, too.

"Where did you learn to cook like this?" she asked.

"I got tired of fast food a few years ago, so I took a course. I dated the teacher, too." He grinned. "I got an A."

"I bet," Alison said dryly, not liking the idea of him with another woman. She had no right to feel that way, yet she couldn't help herself. "I can boil an egg, but beyond that I starve."

"I'll teach you," he volunteered.

He wasn't talking about food, and she knew it.

"I think I'd rather pay Julia Child."

"Thanks a lot, Alison."

"You're welcome." She enjoyed the rest of dinner all the more for having control of the underlying sexual tension. Boy, did it underlie! She could feel the awareness thickening with each glance, each gesture. Jared's face radiated with virile health. At moments, his blue eyes pierced her soul. Her fingers itched to caress his rugged features, and his smile charmed her senses. He was just breathtaking. By the time dinner was over, she could barely look at him. That odd bipolar reaction of heightened awareness combined with crippling shyness was tenfold more powerful with Jared.

Their small talk died an awkward death. Alison wondered what she had said and hoped she hadn't tripped herself up again. Normally, she was careful, but things just popped out around Jared.

She helped him clean up the kitchen. They avoided touching each other. At least she studiously avoided getting close to him while she loaded his dishwasher. He put leftovers into the fridge.

"I'm ready for the tour," she announced, shutting the dishwasher door on the last pot. "I'll just get paper and pencil so I can write down what you want."

Then she would find a magazine picture that had it and be done with Jared Holiday. She hoped.

She got a steno pad and pen out of her tote, then fed the straps of it over one shoulder. She wanted to be able to scoot right out the door as soon as they were finished.

Jared said, "What do you think about the kitchen?"

"I wouldn't touch a thing."

"No. Seriously. It needs new cabinets and flooring. And wallpaper. Maybe paint. Probably you should gut it—"

"I wouldn't touch a thing," Alison repeated.

Jared made a face, then said, "All right. But the dining room needs work."

"I wouldn't touch a thing," Alison said.

"But you haven't seen it yet!"

"We had dinner in it."

"Oh...that's right. Well, it needs work, too."

Alison just stared at him.

"You haven't seen the living room." He led her down the hallway and into the room on the opposite side of the stairs. Flipping on a light, he said, "Now, *this* needs work."

Alison looked at the matched grouping of sofa and chairs, the cherry-wood wall units and tables, and the baby grand piano in one corner. She wanted to ask him if he played, but didn't. Her fingers urged her to go over and try it, although it had been years since she'd played regularly.

"I wouldn't touch a thing."

"How can you say you wouldn't touch a thing for every room?" he demanded.

"Because I could only do it different, not better." *Definitely not better,* she thought.

"Well, I'm tired of the pictures and the pillows.... Let's go upstairs."

She balked at the notion, then reminded herself this was supposed to be innocent. It had better be. If she kept up her stance, he would get the message that she was not the woman for the job. He'd better get the message.

She climbed the stairs behind him, trying not to look at his cute butt. That proved impossible, so she scrutinized it for flaws. The muscles moved gracefully under his trousers, each lift of his legs and feet emphasizing their tautness. His backside would be hard under her hands, powerful with each thrust during lovemaking.

Her body began to throb. Alison began to worry about her control of the sexual tension between her and Jared. She felt very out of control already.

"How many rooms up here?" she asked, her voice cracking.

"Four bedrooms and two baths. One is in the master

bedroom," Jared replied, reaching the last step and turning to wait for her.

She cleared her throat, hoping it would sound normal now that the view was. "Why such a big house? I thought you lived alone."

"I do. I have. But I wanted to buy my permanent house before I was thirty. I made it by two days." He smiled. "It's all part of my life's plan."

"You have a plan for life?"

"Sure. Doesn't everyone?"

"You are efficient."

"I try." He led her to the first room. "Here's guest room number one."

Alison looked in the doorway. "I wouldn't change a thing."

"I was afraid you'd say that."

She did say that about every guest room. This was fun, she thought. Why bother changing a room nobody used, anyway?

"You're not cooperating," Jared complained, before he took her to the last room. His room.

"I'm giving my assessment," she said. "Why waste your money when the house looks fine?"

"But I need a change," he said. "Haven't you ever wanted a change? God, you must. You moved from Chicago to here."

"But that wasn't to change my decor," she answered. "That was to change my life-style."

"So I'm keeping my life-style but changing my decor. I really need the change." Unfortunately, he sounded as though he did. "Here. Look in the last room before you say no."

He opened the door to a room of black-and-white, austere furnishings with an Asian flavor. Touches of mauve and pearl were the only colors, but too little of either relieved the starkness. The whole effect was Spartan and rigid.

"You should have dated the decorator," Alison said.

"It's a thought," he commented.

Alison looked at his bed. It was a mistake. She forgot Spartan and all the rest as she stared at the black silk comforter on the large mattress. She could envision herself naked against it, the silk caressing her flesh as she waited for Jared, like a concubine waiting for an emperor. By the time she was finished with him, he would have no need for other mates, she thought. She would ensure that.

"I wouldn't change a thing," she murmured.

"But I want you to change everything," he said from behind her.

"Why?" she asked in a low voice.

"I don't know," he replied, gazing at her. "Yes, I do. I love you."

The world reeled and bucked, sending her spinning into outer space for one endless moment. "That's impossible."

"I don't think so."

"But why?"

He touched her arms with gentle hands. "Now that I don't know. I just do."

He pulled her to him and kissed her. His mouth was as gentle as his touch, questing and questioning for her response. Alison wanted to deny herself, but the effort was beyond her capabilities. His words rang in her head. Dumping her bag on the floor, she pressed against him, wrapping her arms around his neck. Something vaporized her common sense, and she became the aggressor. Her tongue searched out his, mating with him more frantically. Blood rushed through her veins in a growing heat. A throbbing began deep in her belly. She tugged at his hair, loving the way the strands slid through her fingers.

Jared moaned in the back of his throat and crushed her to him. He kissed her cheeks, her neck, her throat, sending shivers through her body. His hands knotted tightly in her hair as he kissed her again and again. Alison rose on her toes, to settle her lips more intimately on his. She gave herself up to the sensations running rampant inside her. Her breasts ached to feel his touch.

As if he knew her need before she did, his hands cupped her breasts, curving around each globe as if it was made for him. She felt no embarrassment from his touch this time—only heat. Alison moaned when he unbuttoned her blouse and undid her bra. His hands were hot and strong against her skin. He spread tiny, biting kisses across her chest. His fingers stroked her nipples to diamond points. She swayed, her knees turning to water.

His mouth nuzzled one nipple as he lifted her up against him, taking her weight easily. Alison's head dropped back and she closed her eyes, letting her emotions flow through her. He suckled her until she was crying out at the hot pleasure he created inside her. Her skin burned and shivered. Her brain spun. She cradled his head to her, planting fierce kisses in his hair. His male scent of sandalwood cologne and hot need imprinted on her senses. Nothing else mattered. Just Jared. Only Jared. In a moment, she knew he would lay her on that black coverlet and strip her clothes from her until the silk *did* envelop her flesh. Then he would rise above her, naked. Hard and lean. Ready to take her to impossible heights, to end her lonely existence…

Jared was lost in the taste of her, in Alison's fragrance, in her warm, incredibly soft flesh. He had known she would be fantastic. He had known passion would exist like this between them. He had waited years for the unique emotional and physical combination that he felt now. He wanted Alison with every fiber of his being.

The bed was only a few steps away.

Jared lifted his head. Alison's face was flushed with the first throes of desire. Her breasts were beautiful milky globes that fit his hands perfectly. Her nipples were erect.

Lord help him, he thought, because he was about to turn it all away. His body screamed in protest when he tucked her head under his chin and tightened his arms around her back in a platonic hug. He held her, listening to their harsh breathing ease. He had said he loved her, surprising himself as well as her. He had jumped on an emotion too fast—way too fast—even though it felt so right.

"We can't," he said finally.

She stiffened. "What?"

"We can't make love."

When she would have broken the embrace, he held her more tightly. "I want to. God, I want to, Alison, but we're rushing ourselves. In a few more seconds, we wouldn't have been able to stop. You need to know I'm a gentleman."

"I do?"

He chuckled. "Yes, you do. I want no regrets from you. Ever."

"You're right." She began to fix her clothes, although she didn't leave his embrace. When she was finished, she pulled away from him. Her face was rosier than before. "I know you're right.... Well, this is embarrassing.

I wish I could say I didn't mean to throw myself at you, but I'd be lying.''

This was what he liked about her—her straightforwardness. "I'm glad you're not. Throw yourself at me anytime, as long as we get to know each other in the process—"

"We can't," she interrupted, picking up her bag. "I'm just a temporary employee in your office and a temporary decorator."

"You're more than that."

"No. You don't love me, you know."

"I don't?"

She shook her head. "You just got caught up in the moment. We both did."

"It was the *right* moment—"

"It was *a* moment." She smoothed back her hair. "Jared, this attraction between us just won't work."

"I think it will work very well, but it's best to not rush it." He had with his declaration. He'd scared her with it, too. A thought occurred to him. "You think I'm rejecting you." He stepped toward her, his arms outstretched. "Alison...sweetheart."

She evaded him. "I think you were absolutely right about stopping. This is just sex."

"Now I think I'm being rejected."

"No...well, yes...no, not really..." She spun around in a circle and waved a hand. "Dammit! I'm confused and this is a mess."

"The confusion I accept. The mess, no. We just need time. I want to know everything about you—"

"No...there's nothing to know. I'm just an ordinary person, no different from millions of others."

"You are *very* different," he said. "You're unique.

Every time I guess something about you, I guess wrong.''

The panicked expression on her face surprised him. ''You make too much of that sort of thing.''

''I don't think so,'' he replied, puzzled by her reaction. She ought to be flattered that she had a mystique.

''Oh, sure, you do.'' She took his arm and guided him out of the room, while saying, ''Everyone thinks things are mysterious when they're just unfamiliar, that's all.''

''My point exactly. We're unfamiliar with the intimate details of each other's life.''

''Ah, but familiarity breeds contempt.''

He raised his eyebrows. ''Good point. So it's better not to know each other, just go to bed.''

''No, that's not what I'm saying. I'm saying I'm new to your world. That makes me interesting to you. A few more weeks and I'll be just one of the girls.''

He laughed. ''Alison, you will never be just 'one of the girls' at Davis, Hansen and Davis.''

''That is a tough crowd,'' she conceded. ''But I really am no different from any woman in my age group.''

''What are you looking for out of life?'' he asked, when they reached his front door.

She looked blank. ''I—I...''

''See? Most women your age have a goal, have even reached it already, or most of it. Why don't you have a goal? What's shaped you that way? That's what I need to know about you. And you need to know things about me.''

''That's only because I'm new—''

''Don't go there again,'' he said, shuddering, his brain still confused from her argument. He had broken the familiarity loop and he wasn't going back. ''This decorating job will help you to know all about me.''

"I'll just get some more pictures," she began.

"No, there are special things I want for my home that pictures won't cover." He took her hand. "Tell you what. I'll pick you up at your place tomorrow night, and we'll go window-shopping at the mall" He grinned. "I'll use the valet service. I know how that turns you on."

"Oh, no. Coming to my home is impossible."

"No, it's not. I just drive there and voilà!"

"No voilàs, please."

He frowned. She was being too stubborn on the subject of picking her up at home. Suspicions flared. "Do you have a boyfriend? A husband? Is that what all this evasion is about?"

She glared at him. "I am not some run-around! That's a terrible thing to suggest to any woman, that's she's been unfaithful. Especially after we…"

"See why we need to get to know each other much better?" He smiled, very pleased to have his point proven, even if he'd nearly lost his head in his process. "I'll come over tomorrow and pick you up."

"No."

"What now?" he asked, becoming angry with her. She'd gone into his arms as though she belonged there. She had wanted to make love to him. And now she was backing away faster than an elephant from a mouse. What the hell was this?

"Tomorrow's a bad night. I have a—a cooking class."

"I thought you weren't much of a cook."

"Why do you think I need the lessons?"

"I offered to teach you," he said, the conversation details surfacing in his brain.

"And I declined because I said I would pay Julia Child first. Well, I'm paying."

"Not Julia Child."

She gave him a look of disbelief. "No kidding."

He wanted to question her more, but stayed focused on the original quest. "OK, the night after."

"Bad night."

"Alison, you have a choice," he said, finally having his fill of cooking classes and other dodges. "Either you can pick a night to go on a decorating hunt or I can get your address through the temp agency and come drag you out. Don't think I can't get your address. I can. Now, what will it be?"

She glared at him, her mouth a thin line of anger and frustration. He refused to back away from his stance.

Finally she said, "Friday would be fine."

He smiled broadly. "Good."

"Don't be so smug," she said, her tone ice cold. "This will be the fastest decorating job since Samson knocked down the pillars of the Philistine temple. And then I'm out of here. Good night, Jared."

She flung open his front door and strode through it, slamming it behind her with a bang.

"A well-rounded religious background," he mused. "I'll have to put that on the list."

Later that night, he decided, religious knowledge aside, to review his list for his ideal mate. Alison had to have a few of them under her belt by now. Especially after the encounter in his bedroom where he'd admitted his love. She might have stormed out, but she'd left a cyclone of emotions behind.

IDEAL MATE ATTRIBUTES
by Jared Holiday

I. Physical Beauty
- A. Dark-hair, straight Preferably sophisticated style
- B. Doe-like Brown eyes
- C. Exotic Features, delicate
- D. Creamy skin, absolutely unblemished
- E. Large Breasts
- F. Small waist
- G. Long, slender legs
- H. Petite frame, but negotiable as long as it looks good
- I. Two years younger than husband. (Me.)

Jared frowned and crossed out A, C, E, H and I. They were over-rated. He moved to the next section.

II. Intelligence

- A. M.B.A., at least
- B. Attended Ivy League school
- C. Have had at least one scholarship for grade point average
- D. Shrewd in personal finances
- E. Can assess people and situations quickly

He'd have to cross out the whole section if he were honest with himself. Jared decided A and B could go. They got lined. He didn't know what the heck to do with D. He left it alone and moved further down the list.

III. Personal Background

    A. Personal wealth preferable, enough to live comfortably

    B. Parents, relatives have personal wealth/No bums

    C. Family name of some social standing

    D. Race unimportant, but prefer Oriental.

Another section that would have to be axed. D was gone anyway. Maybe if he found some other attributes to take their places. The only ones to fit Alison, unfortunately, weren't attributes. Maybe the next section would have pluses, he thought.

IV. Career

    A. Well along her corporate ladder

    B. Has a commitment to her job

    C. Totally understands his needs with his job

    D. Does not plan to interrupt career for family

A could definitely go. He crossed it out. He frowned at the others. He moved on.

V. Social Abilities

    A. Adapts to any situation

    B. Can talk with anybody about anything, knowledgeably

    C. Thrives on social situations

    D. Loves to entertain; last minute guests are never a problem

    E. Understand the importance of entertaining for husband's career

    F. Will further her husband's cause in any way she can

G. Is active in at least two community organizations

He hated crossing anything out here. Maybe this section needed new attributes to replace the old ones.

VI. Personal Likes and Dislikes

A. Takes great care of her person; always looks
perfect day and night
B. Is a tigress in bed
C. Defers to husband's opinions, career and
needs above her own
D. Wants two children and will be very giving
mother to them
E. Likes nouveau cuisine/cooks like a pro
F. Likes plays
G. Likes symphonies
H. Likes foreign films over domestic
I. Dresses in designer clothes, European flair
J. Likes Jazz over other types of music
K. Generally very upscale in her total outlook
L. Calm nature/prefers smoothing over matters to
fighting

He had a real good feeling about B after tonight. *Extremely* good. He'd work on the rest.

VII. Most important

A. Love is not a requisite for her for marriage
B. She sees the value of good companionship and
sharing similar interests with her husband
C. Although not a proponent of open marriage for

herself, she will turn the occasional blind eye to her husband's outside needs

Jared groaned. This whole section needed revising. Where had his brain been? In the young and egotistical mode. Oh, well.

NOTE: Candidates must reach 90% of attributes for serious consideration.

Jared crossed out the ninety-percent and wrote in seventy. Ninety was too high anyway. Who the hell could make that? Not Alison. And he liked her for that.

No, he thought. He loved her for that.

He put the list away.

Chapter Seven

Alison stared at the pile of Davis, Hansen and Davis folders that needed to be filed daily. It was enormous. On top of it was Jared's billing for the client whose first appointment she had sat in on. Fortunately, a clerk took care of the filing, otherwise Alison would never get around to microfilming.

She'd like to bill Jared, Alison thought darkly. Right in the nose. Leave it to him to create more of a mess in her life. Now she had to get an apartment! In three days!

"Wonderful," she muttered, still disgusted at the conclusion she had come to during her sleepless night.

But what else could she do? How could she explain away her current hotel address? No temp made the kind of money to afford even a modest room at a Holiday Inn. And in his business Jared had detective connections he could tap. She had seen their reports in the short time she'd spent working directly for him. If he wanted to, he could set them on her, should she disappear. Or should she block him even more about her apartment. She had a feeling he would, which was why she'd clammed up last night.

Her boss, Art Mallowan, wouldn't like what she'd gotten herself into.

Art would be easy to cope with, she admitted. Jared wasn't. He loved her—or so he said. Why would a man say that out of the blue? The question had puzzled her all night, which was probably why she couldn't come up with a decent plan of action other than getting an apartment and taking the fib one step further.

He must have been caught up in the heat of the moment, she thought. She knew she had been. Maybe he was one of those guys who blurted out the words in passion, like other men called the wrong name. Maybe Jared said it every time, to every woman he was with.

The notion stung. Stung hard.

Alison swallowed back a sudden lump in her throat. She should be grateful if he didn't mean it. She should be relieved. She glanced at her watch. Four o'clock. Maybe he was back from court.

She went down to his office, surprised to find a small group of lawyers at his open door.

"Congratulations, man!"

"I know you'd make a great one, along with Bill and Margaret. Hey, I'm not taking sides in this. Only one of you wins."

"The committee has a tough choice to make."

Jared's new secretary, a nonthreatening woman in her forties, leaned over her desk and whispered to Alison, "Jared's been nominated as one of three candidates for the open partnership."

"No kidding? That's wonderful!" Alison's heart welled with happiness for him.

"Did you want to see him?" the woman asked.

"I'll come back later," Alison said.

"Just wait a minute. They're all leaving."

The group dispersed a few moments later. Jared stood

in the doorway after accepting his colleagues' felicitations. He looked at Alison and smiled.

"I hear congratulations are in order," Alison said, grinning. "Congratulations."

"I'm only nominated for the job."

"Who cares? It's still great."

"Thanks." He chuckled.

"Can I see you?" she asked.

"Sure. Come in. I want you to look at the wallpaper, anyway."

Alison went into his office. He closed the door behind them, setting off butterflies in her stomach. *OK,* she thought, *just look at the wallpaper.*

It was still too beige.

"I guess it's dry by now," Jared commented.

"I guess so." She frowned. "The paperhanger assured me this was the right color, even the right lot number. The furniture's due this week. We'll see then."

He would see then. Maybe the whole decorating thing would be a moot point.

"At least I'll get my office back," he said, leaning next to the statue of Justice on his desk. He picked it up and stared at it, then smiled and set it down.

"You didn't come here for wallpaper," he said, gazing at her with those damnable, soul-piercing eyes of his.

She wished she hadn't come. What would she say? Did he regret saying he loved her? That was stupid.

On the other hand, if he thought it stupid and embarrassing, he might not want to be around her anymore. And if he wasn't around her anymore, then this whole nonsense would go away.

Did she want it to? *Don't go there,* she thought. She needed this attraction to go away. Fast.

"You really didn't want to say you love me, did you?" she asked boldly.

His face went blank. Finally, he said, "Yes, I did mean it."

"But you don't want to mean it."

"Am I feeling like I'm out on a limb? Sure. You haven't said it back."

Definitely don't go there, she thought. "Then we're in an embarrassing situation. I'll just finish your office, and we can call it even."

"What are you hiding, Alison?"

"I'm not hiding anything," she managed to say in an innocently surprised voice. She also managed to not gape at him, which would be a dead giveaway that he was right. "You're the one making outrageous pronouncements. I thought you'd want an out, and frankly, *I'm* a little embarrassed by the whole thing, so I wouldn't mind an out, either."

"I may not believe in love at first sight," he said. "And I may be under some delusion, but you really are evading contact. I don't think it has anything to do with our attraction to each other. Or how I'm feeling about you. Why don't you want me to know where you live?"

"It's not that," she began.

"Then tell me."

"I just think this is becoming too complicated."

"Bull. Why don't you want me any closer in *any* way?"

"I'm a private person—"

"Why don't you answer the simplest of questions in a straightforward manner?"

"I do."

"No, you don't. Why are you working as a temp when you have other skills you avoid using?"

"It's not that—"

"Why don't you want a permanent job, then, in this field?"

"It's not what I'm looking for—"

"You're not looking for anything. Why is that?"

Alison's mind raced even faster to come up with an acceptable answer. Instead, it veered in another direction. "I'm feeling pressured by you about our relationship."

"*Bzzz*. Wrong answer. If that had been your true response, it would have been your instant response."

"You're confusing me," she said, feeling trapped.

"I shouldn't be able to, not unless you're already confused. Go back to work, Alison. I'll see you Friday evening."

She opened her mouth to protest, then realized anything she said could and would be used against her. "You're very good at this, aren't you?"

"The best."

She smiled. "Don't bet on it."

She walked out of his office with great dignity. Better to leave as a lion than as the scared rabbit she felt like. She probably didn't fool him, but at least she felt better about her exit. The problem was she never should have made an entrance.

After work, she called her real boss from a pay phone. Art Mallowan had been at the bureau for over twenty years. He'd survived and thrived under four White House administrations, oodles of budget cuts and other bureaucratic obstacles to getting the job done. He'd taken Alison under his wing and put her on a new project to ensure that relocated protection witnesses weren't cut loose after a few years.

"About time you checked in," the gravelly voice complained over the phone line.

"I know." Alison smiled, feeling as though her world was back to normal just hearing Mallowan's dulcet tones.

"So what's the story there in Philly?" he asked. "I've got some people who have to be moved."

"It's expensive," she replied. "I want to check farther out in the suburbs."

"The old underworld's dead there," Mallowan said. "Now's a good time to get people into the Northeast. The Southwest looks like Chicago's east side. I need you to move on, too. We've got the North Carolina project hanging. How long will you be?"

"That's the question, Art." Alison sighed. "I'm afraid I've bungled it a little." An understatement if she'd ever made one. "I'm going to leave questions behind if I don't finish this up properly."

"How did you bungle it?" Art's voice was cold and curious at the same time.

"I have to decorate a guy's house."

Dead silence reigned over the telephone. Then laughter roared across the miles from Washington. "I gotta hear this one."

She told him everything, except about the personal attraction she felt for Jared. She wasn't about to mention that.

"Sounds like the guy's got a hard-on for you."

"Art!"

"I *meant* that he's not giving up on you. Boy, but you have a dirty mind. When did you develop that?"

"Oh..." She ignored his question. The answer was too damn easy. "The problem is, I just can't vanish without leaving a lot of questions behind. Questions he's in a position to pursue for answers.''

"Yeah, he'd probably feel scammed by his 'decorator' and go to the police. Alison, you've been my best field agent since we instituted this program for long-term living venues. Federal monies can support these people for only so long and then they have to support themselves. We have to ensure they'll be psychologically matched up with a community where they can stay hidden, securely and comfortably. You live their lives. Your participation's invaluable. You're not losing your edge, are you?''

I hope not, she thought. "No. I just walked into someone who thrives on details. It was bound to happen.''

"Well, get his house decorated and get the hell out.'' Art chuckled grandly, more amused than annoyed by her predicament. "I'd love to see you surrounded by swatches, but I'm too ticked at you right now.''

"It's magazine pictures, not swatches.''

"Well, hustle it up. And Alison?''

"Yes?''

"Don't forget to do your real job while you're at it.''

"I'd love to. In the meantime, I need an apartment.''

"What?''

She held the phone out while Art cursed roundly. When he wound down, she put the receiver back to her ear. "I need an apartment, Art. Don't ask why. It's complicated, but if I don't have one the questions will start again. Can you get me anything here before Friday?''

"You better give me a report the likes of which would put a smile on Hoover's face.''

"I promise you will be dancing on your desk.''

"I'd better be. Call me back in three hours. I'll have a place for you then.''

"Bless you, Art. Bless you."

"Yeah, well…just hustle it, girl."

She hoped he wasn't prophetic. But she hung up the phone with a sigh of relief. He hadn't cremated her over the mess she'd created. But she had to get out of this, somehow.

That night she inspected her new apartment, her footsteps echoing eerily off the bare hardwood floors in the empty room. Good, she thought, the one-bedroom place was more than adequate for her needs. This ought to satisfy Jared.

Two days later, she held the Justice statue as she'd promised, protecting it from the burly movers. The furniture was perfect. She glanced at the waterfall picture and nodded to herself. Perfect. Even the slight difference in the wallpaper didn't clash so far as she could tell.

"What do you think?" she asked, turning to the one who could tell.

"Great," Jared said proudly. He pushed a chair a few inches to the left. "Great job, Alison. I love it. I think the clients will, too."

Several lawyers poked their heads in and oohed and aahed. Even Robert Davis smiled as he looked around Jared's new office.

"I like this," Robert said.

"Alison put it together," Jared said.

"She did?" The senior lawyer whipped around to gaze at her. "Very nice, young lady."

"Thank you," she murmured.

One job down, one to go. She was on the road out of Philadelphia and out of Jared's life.

Her heart felt heavy. She ignored it.

JARED STARED at the lawn chairs in horror.

"I'm ready to go," Alison announced, after getting

her jacket from her closet.

"Alison, you only have two chairs—two *lawn* chairs," he said, finally finding his voice after saying hello at the door and stepping into her nearly empty apartment.

"And a radio. Don't forget that."

"But you're a decorator! Where's the decorating?"

"Oh." She shrugged. "You've heard about the shoemaker's kids going barefoot? Same principle here."

"But..."

"Come on. You wanted this jaunt, now you've got it."

After that not-very-auspicious announcement, she took his arm and led him out of her apartment.

"You're practically homeless!" he exclaimed, still shocked by her lack of belongings.

She chuckled. "Jared, you exaggerate."

"Two lawn chairs and a radio, and *I* exaggerate?"

She waved a hand. "I just moved here, remember. I'm still settling in."

As he drove to the mall, her words mollified him a little. But only a little. No wonder she didn't want him here. How could she live so on the edge like this? It was inhuman. His heart broke for her. He'd helped women all his career....

He was helping Alison, he thought. He might have given her the decorating jobs for selfish reasons, but his instincts had been more accurate than he'd known. He'd get her more work, help her more, make her a rich woman. A very rich woman.

"You're quiet," she said, breaking into his musings.

"Just thinking."

"About what you saw in my apartment?"

"Yes. Alison—"

"Jared, it's not a big deal. My furniture just hasn't arrived yet."

"It hasn't?" he echoed.

"I told you, I'm still settling in."

Her furniture not arriving explained some. But a lot more needed explaining, like why she'd been working for Davis, Hansen and Davis for a month and still didn't have her furniture.

She was all-business, taking notes while they window-shopped for his new house decor. He'd expected a more leisurely time, the two of them strolling along, just looking and getting ideas. He would take her elbow to keep her close to him in the crowd of shoppers, only the crowd was thin this Friday evening. He hadn't expected it in a mall this massive.

He took her hand instead. Her palm was soft, warm, sending his blood pumping through his body....

Alison slipped her hand from his.

Jared frowned. "Alison—"

"Do you like this vase?" she asked, picking up a large one from a store display and holding it up.

"Where would you put it?" he asked, wondering why she even looked at the hideous thing.

"I was thinking of doing your living room in Russian...."

Her voice sounded more tentative than firm. But the notion of bright red and black mosaics and balalaikas hanging from the walls appalled him. "I like my literature Russian, not my living room."

"OK." She set down the vase.

This time she walked far enough away from him that he would have to lunge for her hand.

"I don't bite," he growled, feeling like a pariah.

She glanced at him. "Why would you say that?"

"Because you're way over there."

"Someone has to be. Oh, look. Scandinavian. Nice, clean lines. Stark and cool. That's you, Jared." She hurried toward the store.

"I thought I was complex and hot," he muttered to himself, his ego pricked badly.

Inside the store, Alison moved from sofa to chair to table. The pale birch wood and Arctic white cushions looked uncomfortable at best, forbidding at worst.

"What about this?" she asked, holding up a wrought-iron reindeer knickknack.

"It's OK," he said politely.

Alison wrote in her little notebook. Jared commented politely about several more things she pointed out as possibilities for his house. Her growing enthusiasm infected him. He pushed his concerns and puzzlements aside, to enjoy this time with her.

"I like this lamp," Alison said, touching a Southwestern-style fixture in yet another shop.

"What? For the Norwegian living room?" he asked, teasing.

"Oh...oh Lord, yes." She grinned. "It would be perfect with that bright green wall unit we saw."

"I think it was bright red."

"OK, so these pinks and blues would blend right in."

"I think I'm running away from home," Jared vowed. *Right to her apartment,* he thought. She had an extra lawn chair. And she had to have a bed.

They stopped at a coffee bar. Jared did his total yuppie route with a skinny mocha cream and Colombian, while Alison ordered an herbal tea decaf.

"This an eating day or noneating?" he asked, not sure where she was in her schedule.

"Eating."

"Two *biscotti*," he added to the server.

Alison laughed. "What would you have done if it was a noneating day for me?"

"Ordered one *biscotto* and tortured you."

"What a nice guy you are."

They sat down at a table just outside the coffee bar. Alison totaled up her list of possibles for his house. "I have twenty-three items here."

Jared frowned, then sipped his mocha cream. The hot, barely sweet chocolate coffee slid down his throat like aged whiskey. "You didn't write down everything we looked at, did you?"

"Everything you said you liked. By the way, you have a coffee mustache."

"Want to lick it off?"

Alison looked heavenward, then murderously at him. "Jared, this isn't a lark."

"It isn't? OK." After he wiped his lip with his napkin—a disappointment after his first suggestion—he put up his hand. "I promise I'll be good. Sure you didn't want to lick it off?"

"Jared!"

"OK...but I still think—"

"One more crack out of you and that mocha cream goes right in your lap."

"Hot dog! I can't wait for you to lick it off *there*."

"Jared!" Alison exclaimed, her face turning rosy. She glanced at the people sitting at surrounding tables. No one paid attention to them. "OK, so I walked straight into that one. Here. Look at the damn list."

She shoved her notepad his way. He grinned at her annoyance, then glanced at the list. Half of the items on it sent alarm bells ringing in his head. "I was only kidding about some of these."

"You were?"

"Of course I was. Alison, why would I want Scandinavian, Queen Anne and Mission Oak in my living room?"

"You seemed to like eclectic."

"There's eclectic and then there's insane."

"I'm only trying to give you what you want." She wagged a finger at him. "I told you pictures were better."

"Not this time," he said firmly. "I just confused you, playing around."

"Pictures would be better," she warned.

"But not as much fun. Look at how we're getting to know each other."

"I know you have no clue what you want."

"I have every clue," he assured her. "I know I want you."

Alison's eyes went wide.

"Drink your coffee, honey," he said, sipping his.

"I ought to put my *tea* where the sun don't—"

"Be sweet now," Jared said, interrupting her threat. Although it did have possibilities.

"Oh, drink your mocha *latte,* skinny decaf," Alison advised, in the sweetest of voices, "and let's get on with the useless, why-bother-other-than-to-have-fun decorator's dream tour."

Jared chuckled.

"OK," she said later, when they were in Niemann-Marcus. "Do you want the olive leather wing chair or don't you?"

"I don't know," he mused. "What do you think?"

"I think my foot's going to follow my tea. What about the conquistador painting there?"

"Love it, just love it." Actually he did, the painting being a copy of a grand master's. A fairly good copy, too.

"OK," she said, noting it down.

"But it depends on the rest of the decor," he said.

She scratched it off the list.

The store announced it was closing in five minutes.

"Saved," Alison said, suddenly cheerful.

Jared sighed. "I didn't want this night to end."

"Me, neither. I'm just thrilled with window-shopping on a Friday night, especially when I'm with you. It's right up there with getting a root canal."

"Sarcasm becomes you."

"I was being sardonic."

"That explains it."

She chuckled. "Can we go to the valet service now?"

"You really like that, don't you?"

"It's wonderful. I really have no life, do I?"

He laughed, knowing she loved the whole notion of mall valet service. Tonight they hadn't needed it, but he couldn't resist rubbing in her last visit to the mall. Besides, the valet service seemed to give him good luck. They'd kissed for the first time afterward.

So he was stretching it, he thought.

Still, he was pleased with tonight's work. She might have had moments when she'd wanted to kill him, but he had learned a lot about her. Maybe he ought to be less pleased and more worried about her personal life, he decided, remembering two lawn chairs, a radio and unanswered questions.

The furniture not arriving sounded lamer and lamer. He doubted she had any furniture; nor could she prob-

ably afford any on her salary. How she was paying for
the apartment was a mystery to him. He had to know
what had brought her to this pass. Something she said
on Labor Day surfaced.

"You said your mother has passed away," he began,
once they were in his car and on the way to her place.

"I did?"

"Yes." He frowned. "On your first day at Davis,
Hansen and Davis. You made a comment that your de-
ceased mother would be upset with what you were typing."

"Oh. Oh, yes. What about it?"

She sounded too matter-of-fact. "That must have been
terrible. Was she killed in an accident?"

"Well...she was ill, and she had an accident."

"And your dad's gone, too."

"Yes, he died three years ago after a long illness. I
have a brother—"

"I thought you said you had no relatives," he interrupted, confused.

"I did?"

"Yes, you did. You said you were an orphan."

She shrugged. "Well, I'm not."

"Then why did you say you were?"

"Were what?"

"An orphan!"

"I couldn't have. I've got a mother and a brother."

"But you just said your mom was killed in an accident."

"I said she was ill and she *had* an accident. I never
said she died."

Jared growled in his throat, frustrated. He was positive
she had denied having a family. Certainly, she'd said her
mother was gone. He glanced over at her. She stared out

the front window, her profile calm and cool in the dashboard light. Maybe he hadn't heard her right about her family.

No. He had. So why would a person deny having relatives? What would be the point?

His own family hadn't been great, but he didn't deny their existence. And he loved his cousins. Maybe her relatives were worse. Maybe she had moved because of horrendous family problems. How she must have suffered, he thought, as the puzzle clicked into place. How she must still be suffering.... How much emotional baggage did she carry with her?

Another time, another woman, and he would have been scared away. But Alison's problems, whatever they were, didn't frighten him. He was ready to help her however he could.

"Where do I turn for your place?" Jared asked, pulling into an apartment complex.

"Ah..." Alison gazed at the mishmash of buildings sprawling before them. "I don't know."

He stepped on the brakes hard. The car jerked to a stop. He rounded on her. "What do you mean, you don't know? How can you not know where you live?"

Alison glared at him. "It's a big complex. I still get lost sometimes, OK? I'm not perfect. If you give me a few moments to orient myself, I'll tell you...wait a minute! You have directions I gave you earlier. Just use them."

He felt in his pockets, then looked out the window. "I think I lost them."

"And you're yelling at me?"

"But you live here. I don't."

"A technicality." She was silent for a long moment,

then said, "Just drive around, and we'll find it. This road is the main one. I think."

Jared took his foot off the brake and put his car in motion again. "How long have you lived here?"

"Not long." In a wry tone, she added, "Not long enough, it looks like. Turn left here."

"Unless you moved in yesterday, you really ought to know your way around by now."

"Are you always so critical?"

"Me, critical?" he yelped, outraged by the suggestion. "You live in an apartment complex for months and can't find your own place. What do you expect me to say?"

"I haven't lived here for months."

"How long then?"

"Awhile. I don't know exactly. Turn right here."

She was back to the flower-child image full force. He'd thought she'd dropped it long ago. She was more of an enigma to him than ever.

Alison asked him to turn onto several more access roads. Each turn dead-ended, however, in a parking lot edged by buildings. She guided him out, only to have them dead-end again.

"What the hell is this?" Jared finally asked in frustration, as they made a U-turn out of another lot. "Alison—"

"I'm looking, I'm looking," she said, looking. "I don't like to drive at night, so I'm not used to finding my apartment in the dark, that's all. As soon as we see my yellow Fiero, we'll know we're there."

"Alison!" He couldn't believe she'd been looking for her car all this time.

"What?" She turned to him, her eyes wide and innocent.

Jared sighed. He saw no sense in arguing further. He'd lose. Maybe if they attacked this from another angle, they'd have success. "What's your apartment number?"

"*Q* 34. We haven't found the *Q* building yet. I *have* looked."

"I don't think we will find it." He pointed to a sign on the side of one of the buildings. "This is building 21. The others here are numbered, too."

"That can't be," Alison said, frowning. "My building begins with a letter. I *know* that."

"I've got to be in the *Twilight Zone*," Jared commented, steering them back to the complex's main road. He knew he could find that; he'd been on it six times already.

He stopped at a direction sign for the complex. The buildings were all laid out on it, each one marked with a number, not a letter, the reverse of Alison's apartment number. Or what she said was her apartment number.

"I guess it must be 34-*Q*," she said sheepishly as she gazed at the map.

"It can't be. There is no number-34 building," he said. "And the individual apartments in each building only go up to *J*."

"No *Q?* No 34?"

"Nope."

"What the hell is this?" Alison demanded.

"My question exactly."

"Hey!" She leaned across him and pointed to a legend at the bottom of the sign. "This is *Fox Meadows* apartments. I live at *Fox Hollow* apartments."

Something in his brain, which had been momentarily in the throes of delight with her closeness, popped at this piece of news. "What? Why didn't you tell me?"

She straightened away from him, a loss he felt even

in his fury. She said, "I didn't pay any attention to the entrance sign. Besides, you acted like you knew where you were going."

"Don't put the blame on me," he said.

"Why don't we get past this and go to my apartment?"

Her common sense nearly toppled his shredding control. He tromped on the gas pedal, spinning out of the maze in record time. Just down the road was her own apartment development. That the two complexes looked eerily alike and had eerily similar names, obviously part of a large new community, didn't pacify him. He felt confused, bewildered and stupid. *Batting one thousand,* he thought.

Alison, to make matters worse, directed him to her place without a single detour.

"Thank you for an interesting evening," she said.

"We're not finished," he said, knowing he needed something to rectify this disaster. "I'll pick you up tomorrow. If I can find this damn place again."

She tapped her notebook. "I've got plenty of ideas here. I'm just fine."

"We haven't even begun on the bedrooms yet," he informed her, feeling oddly as if he was the decorating expert rather than she. Maybe he was still confused, bewildered and stupid from the apartment search. He bet he would feel this way for a long time.

"I can't tomorrow—"

"Cancel it," he said. "Whatever you have to do can wait. I'll pay you extra."

"I don't want or need money!" she snapped indignantly. "And I don't take orders from you."

Somewhere a fragment of logic rose that warned him not to turn dominant male. "I'm not arguing with you,

Alison. I'm asking you to do the job I hired you for. As a businessperson, I expect you to do what's necessary to perform the job. Tomorrow is Saturday, our best day to do the work. Therefore it's necessary.''

She said nothing for so long he thought she'd turned to stone. It wouldn't surprise him, not with the way the evening had become an avalanche of calamity from one wrong turn.

''Thank you, Jared, for also reminding me of the job,'' she said finally. ''Good night.''

She got out of the car and shut the door a little too gently for his taste. If she'd slammed it, he might have felt reassured, but Alison had been too cool. That worried him.

''I'll be here at ten,'' he shouted, after rolling down his side window. ''And I'll be waiting.''

She opened her front door and walked inside. Just before she shut the door he could have sworn she made an all-American gesture of defiance.

Naa, he thought, shaking his head. *Not Alison.*

Chapter Eight

Alison called in sick on Saturday.

Well, technically, she thought. She'd left her apartment before Jared arrived. But that was her version of calling in sick for the decorating job. After his little macho tirade, he didn't deserve better.

She had real work to do, anyway.

Alison drove through the New Jersey suburbs of Philadelphia, the little towns of the state's southern half all blending together along the roads. She liked the quiet atmosphere and the occasional farms dotted here and there. She knew Jared's cousin Michael lived somewhere around here but couldn't remember exactly where. The area looked less expensive than the western suburbs, and according to the Houses for Sale ads in the newspaper, the homes *were* less expensive than where she was staying on the other side of the city.

She stopped at a mall and window-shopped, this time for sheer pleasure. Prices were definitely better, the shops less upscale. Twenty miles shouldn't make such a difference, even with this area, just across the Delaware River, yet it did. The land was more flat, too. She wondered if the bureau would be wise to settle witnesses into a new life in Jersey. It would be more affordable for them, certainly. But how were the jobs and how was the pay? What were the schools like? And the people?

She left the mall and drove around, not yet willing to go back to her apartment. Its stark emptiness grated on her nerves, and she wished she was back in a familiar hotel room. At least that didn't seem to ask for more from her.

And then there was Jared. She could only envision his reaction when he hadn't found her waiting dutifully for him. No, she wasn't *near* ready to go home again.

A large banner strung across a main street announced a marching-band competition. Besides the piano, she had played clarinet in her high-school band, but they'd never marched. Music had once been a big part of her world. Funny the turns life took. Curious, Alison sought out the football field where the competition was being held.

The place was mobbed. She paid to get in, paid for a program, paid for a fifty-fifty chance at a door prize. She could have paid for several more things but skipped them, although all the "hits" to the pocketbook amused her.

"Why isn't there a football game?" she asked someone, remembering how her high-school fall Saturdays had been spent.

"It's the school's 'Bye' week, so there's no game here today," replied a helpful neighbor in the stands. "Usually, the band competitions start in the evenings, but we have sixteen bands today so it started early."

"Wow." Alison was awed already.

She looked around the packed stands. Blocks of people wore the same shirt that declared them loyal to one band or another. But the kids! She was amazed at the high-school bands' performances of quick-moving drills played to music. Best wishes were announced before each band performed—some poignant, some joking and all obviously from parents, relatives and friends. The color guards, with their flags, sabers, rifles and echoes of ancient pageantry, added to the mix. Different parts of the audience would cheer uproariously while a band performed its drill, to the amusement of the rest of the crowd. One group of parents had horns and noisemakers, bemusing the rest of the parents' groups with their "homer" enthusiasm.

Alison grinned at the community spirit. She found herself wishing something like this had been around when she had been in school. More, she wished she had a true place in this crowd, rather than being here as an observer. She wished she had a child, home, hearth, plus Saturdays filled with marching-band competitions or footballs games or other family activities. Weekly food shopping. Painting the fence. Planting daffodils. Washing the dog.

Alison sighed hours later when the last band marched off the field. She might have found communities for the witness-protection program, but more and more she also found things missing in her own life. Things she had never missed before. Maybe she *was* losing her edge.

All the way home thoughts of Jared grew in her mind, thoughts she'd suppressed for most of the day. Somehow he'd become entangled in her longings for a normal life. He had gotten under her defenses, and she could no longer shut him out.

She pulled into her building's parking lot and immediately wanted to pull out again. Jared's car sat in her visitors' slot. He sat in the car.

His driver's-side door opened, and he shot out before she could do more than think of turning around. So much for not being spotted. Gritting her teeth and screwing up her courage, she parked her car in her slot. She got out as casually as she could.

"Where the hell were you?" he demanded.

"At a high-school marching-band competition," she replied.

He stopped dead, clearly flummoxed. "A marching-band competition?"

She nodded. It occurred to her that a man who would wait all day and half the night for a woman might not have a healthy attitude. The words *Obsessed* and *Stalker* came to mind. "Why did you wait all this time? That's not good, Jared. In fact, it's downright scary."

"Scary?" He thrust his fingers through his hair in frustration. "You break a date. You're gone all day with no word, and you call *me* scary?"

"I told you I couldn't do today."

"You couldn't miss a marching-band competition? Whose was it, anyway?"

"Ah..." Damn, but she couldn't remember the name of the school. "It's only held once a year."

Surely that was true. Maybe they did them every week.

"Oh," he said, stymied. "Well, I didn't mean to scare you. I haven't been here all day and half the night, either. If you had a phone, I would have called until I got hold of you. Since you don't, I've been back and forth. I was concerned about you and whether you were all right."

Alison blushed, ashamed of her defiance. It seemed so petty now when he must have been worried about her. Thank goodness the dark night kept him from seeing her red face.

"I'm sorry," she said. "Would you like to come in for tea?"

He ran his fingers through his hair again. "OK."

She unlocked her apartment, and they went inside. Alison flipped on the light switch. The lawn chairs sat in stark relief to the bare white walls.

"I've got to do something about this place," she muttered.

"When's your furniture due in?" Jared asked.

Furniture due in? She remembered last night's conversation. "Oh, I'm not sure yet. I have to check with the storage company."

"Didn't you talk to them when you first got here?"

She should have had Art arrange for a furnished apartment, Alison thought, disgusted at herself for yet another example of carelessness. She bet that old scoundrel in D.C. had thought of it and was laughing up his sleeve. "I did. But there're a lot of costs to moving, so some things had to wait."

He took out a checkbook.

"Put that away," Alison said sternly, walking into her kitchen. Turning on the light switch revealed it was as stark and bare as the living room. At least she had basic cookware and dining ware. She set her large tote bag on the counter next to the stove and began making tea.

Jared sat at her card table, his checkbook still out. "Look, you've done the work for my office, and I haven't paid you yet—"

"Yes, you have. You wrote all those checks to the paperhangers and the furniture store."

"But not to you personally. You can't tell me you got a cut from the others. I know you didn't."

The cut was a nice idea, she admitted. She wished she'd thought to say it first and let him think she had made money already. "I did this as a favor to you, Jared. I'd feel like a crook if I took the money."

"Forget it, Alison." He wrote a check. "You'll take the money."

"No," she said firmly. "I won't."

He came over to her, check in hand and determination in his gaze. Those blue eyes gleamed fiercely with it. She braced herself to not accept the check, knowing she would be a complete hypocrite if she did. He must have sensed her resistance because before she could stop him, he opened her bag to shove the check inside.

For one endless second, he stared at the contents of her purse, then reached in and pulled out her government-issue .38 pistol. He held it up gingerly. Alison groaned. She always carried the gun when she was "on duty." Today was a workday. She preferred her purse to her body for concealment because the gun always looked like a third breast under her armpit or a tumor growth on her back if she wore it there. Wearing it at her ankle was out for obvious reasons: jeans were too tight and she never wore trousers.

"Alison," he began.

"Put it back," she said, defeated. Now she was totally exposed.

"You're in a great deal of trouble, aren't you?"

She sighed, thinking of what Art would say about this. "Yes."

"I knew it. I knew something was wrong," he said. "You—you've broken the law, haven't you?"

"Oh, no." Even with the tears gathering in her eyes, she laughed at the irony of that notion. "Lord, no, Jared. I haven't broken any laws. I couldn't."

"Someone's after you, then. You're in hiding from them because you're in great danger if they find you."

"You've read too many mysteries."

"Not this time. Alison, sweetheart." He wrapped his

arms around her, hugging her to him in a tight embrace. The side of her pistol was cold ice against her back, not the most comfortable of feelings, especially in the hands of an amateur.

"This is not healthy," she muttered, pushing against him until he let her go.

She took the gun from him and checked the trigger lock, deliberately pointing the weapon toward an outside wall as she did. He hadn't managed to undo the lock, thank goodness. She put the gun back in her bag.

"Alison, tell me what's happened to you," Jared said softly.

He was so sweet, she thought, so wonderful to care. Only he would kill her if he knew the truth. And she couldn't reveal it, not if she wanted to salvage any part of this.

The kettle whistled. She turned it off and poured boiling water into a teapot, letting the tea steep. Then she turned to him. "No."

"I want to help you."

"Jared, you're sweet, so sweet." She sighed and told him what truth she could. "There's nothing to tell. I'm not in trouble. I promise."

"Then why do you carry a gun?"

"Lots of people do," she replied, taking the teapot over to the card table. "I'm a woman who lives alone. I feel I need extra protection, that's all. Your brain works overtime, you know that?"

"You're the one with the gun." He carried over the mugs she'd left on the counter. "You said once that you could shoot the wings off a fly. Can you really?"

"Yes. I don't think anyone should have a gun unless they know how to use it expertly."

"Your having a gun is scary."

She laughed, knowing she was one of the least scary people to have a gun, compared to millions of consumers with second-amendment fervor. "I promise never to use it."

"Then why have it?"

She poured tea into mugs, trying to delay answering until she actually thought of one. "I told you, I'm a woman alone, and I want protection. A gun is the best way for me to provide it."

"But you promised not to use it, so what good is it?"

She sipped her tea. It wasn't quite brewed enough. That figured. "I promise not to use it unless my life's in danger, OK?"

"You said 'Never' before."

Lord help her, she thought. "Jared, you know what I meant."

"You're in trouble," he said again. "I know it."

"No. I'm not. Please believe me, Jared."

He reached across the table and took her hand, his fingers hot and strong against her skin. "Alison, let me help you. What kind of trouble is it?"

She should have followed her own advice to just decorate his place and get out. But no, her feminine ire had to kick in when he became autocratic.

She pulled her hand from his and raised it, since it was her right one. "I swear that I am not in any kind of trouble...." Just with her boss, Art, she thought. "Or anything nefarious, or anything out of—" she paused again, knowing that to say "out of the ordinary" would be untrue "—that's illegal or unethical."

There, she decided. Free and clear. Then she remembered the decorator fib. OK, so presenting herself as having worked in that business wasn't true. But it wasn't a big lie...OK, so it was. But she had learned her lesson.

"You're lying," Jared said, no doubt reading her mind. "You are in trouble somewhere."

"I'm not!" She leaned forward, determined to put him off track. "Jared, you are wrong about me. I'm in no trouble, no danger from anyone."

Except him, and that was emotional danger.

"Alison. Nobody...*nobody* lives like this if they're not in trouble."

Alison gave up. "You are the most stubborn man I have ever met."

"I'm not being stubborn. You're hiding something and I'm concerned."

"Jared, drink your tea. It's been a long day." She sipped hers to make the point, but the tea tasted too sour and flat in her mouth.

"Answer me one question, just one," he said. "Will you tell me everything about your life? Right now?"

Alison glared at him, knowing he had trapped her. "No."

Jared sat back and smiled triumphantly. "See? You're in trouble."

"No kidding," she muttered under her breath.

No kidding.

NOW HE KNEW, Jared thought, eyeing Alison across the card table. Oh, he might not know the details, but he knew the root of Alison's often evasive and odd behavior.

She was in trouble.

He didn't think she had broken a law. First off, who would work in a law office if she had had that in her background? Maybe he'd better take that back, he acknowledged, remembering a few disbarred attorneys with whom he was acquainted. But he didn't think Alison had lied about herself. She tended to not answer tough questions rather than try to bluff her way through them.

She had a gun.

The notion of Alison with a gun frightened him—especially when she had taken it from him and checked it. She'd looked so calm, so collected, so...professional.

She couldn't be on the other side of the law. All his instincts couldn't be that wrong about her.

No, she needed help.

She was stubborn and elusive. He wondered how to tell her he was staying tonight to protect her, without her bolting. He wondered how to tell her a lot of things without her bolting. Slowly, very slowly.

He knew of only one way to stay at a woman's apartment without arousing suspicions. He grinned. Well, they'd arouse something, but he wouldn't complain about that.

He took her hand again and kissed it. "I won't ask any more questions, Alison. I promise."

She smiled with a little too much relief.

"But I didn't promise not to be concerned for you and help you," he added, just to clarify the issue.

"But I don't need help!" she exclaimed, glaring at him. "What do I have to do to convince you? Dance a jig? Scream it from the rooftops? Run naked through Central Park?"

"That's in New York. Here you would run naked through Fairmount Park." He grinned. "And tempting as that might be to view, I think not. I wouldn't like other men to see your luscious body."

"My body is flat as an ironing board," she retorted. "Dammit, Jared, that's enough, OK? I thank you for your concern *even though I don't need it,* and I think it's time to go.''

"No," he said, immediately reaching for her. "Don't leave, Alison. Don't be scared off—"

She pulled away from him. "I meant you, not me."

"Oh." He cleared his throat. "That brings us to a little problem. I'm not going."

"You're not going?" she echoed, looking blankly at him.

"I'm not going until you're safe," he said. "I thought about seducing you so you wouldn't realize I was protecting you. Not that I wouldn't mean to make love— *make love, not sex,*" he added hastily. "But my ultimate goal would be to protect you from whatever's out there looking for you. I think now that would be less than honest—"

Alison's head banged down on the card table. Mugs rattled, the tea sloshing dangerously near the lip of each. Facedown on the tabletop, she said, "Can I kill him, Lord? You know it would be self-defense."

"Alison," Jared said, concerned she was having a breakdown and concerned about the weapon in her purse. In her condition, who knew what she might do?

She raised her head, her face awash with exhaustion. "Jared, go home. Please. I'm perfectly fine. No one will hurt me—except you." She braced her hands on the card table, leaned forward and shouted in his face, "You are making me crazy!"

She sat back in her chair. Silence reigned.

Jared eyed her, wondering if her outburst was due to frustration at him. It seemed genuinely so. He didn't want to upset her further, yet he couldn't leave her in physical danger, nor in this emotional state. He said the only thing he could think of. "Good tea."

"Thank you." She sighed. "Look, you have some-how gotten the wrong impression of me."

"I don't think so."

She glared. He decided that shutting up was the better part of valor at the moment.

"I *know* so," she continued. "I do not need your protection. Clearly, I have my own very effective pro-tection. And I only have it because I am a woman who lives alone. I live in places where having a Doberman isn't feasible, so I got the next best thing. You've been a mystery fan too long, Jared, and that's all there is to *your* theories about me, OK? Now go home and get some rest. It's late and tomorrow will bring you a better perspective."

She sounded almost convincing. *Almost.* Unfortu-nately, she left too many unanswered questions for him to believe her. He could sense fear in her. He felt she was driving him away to protect him from the danger she was in. She was so sweet and so misguided.

"All right," he said, trying to smile innocently, to throw her off the track of a plan forming in his head. "I see your reasoning—"

"Thank goodness!" She smiled back at him, so hap-pily that he wanted only to wrap his arms around her.

"Now promise me that tomorrow you will be here and we will go shopping for my house."

"Oh, I promise." She raised her right hand in the three-fingered Scout salute. "I won't go anywhere, Jared. I'll be right here, eager to get the job done. In fact, I promise I'll do your house over in record time."

He didn't like the sound of that, but he let it go. He rose. "I'll be here at eight tomorrow morning."

"I'll be here."

She looked and sounded so relieved that Jared nearly

changed his mind. Ultimately he wanted a calm Alison. He didn't think she would use a gun, but he didn't want to know for sure.

He walked to her front door. She walked beside him. Her perfume swirled through his senses, telling him he was a fool for not trying to seduce her and worrying about honesty later.

No. Honesty was better. Dammit.

"Jared, I really do appreciate your concern for me." Alison said, after she opened her front door. Cool October air circulated around them. "I hope you do understand that it's not necessary."

"I understand."

She rose and kissed him on the cheek. "Thank you. Thank you for everything."

Trust first, then *sex,* he told himself, while resisting the urge to kiss her senseless. His flesh burned where her lips had touched.

He smiled and kissed her cheek. God, he thought, her skin was so soft, like satin. "Good night, Alison."

He went outside into that chill night, resisting the urge to ruin any progress he'd made.

He turned on the Beamer's motor and deliberately revved the engine. Alison watched from her doorway. He turned on his headlights and sounded his horn, backed out of the slot and drove out of her parking lot. In his rearview mirror, he caught a glimpse of her still in her doorway, making sure he was gone.

She must have a lot to hide, he thought.

He drove around the complex, then back to her parking lot. He shut off the lights, then the car motor when he was close enough to pull into a slot a few spaces down from her own. Her living-room light was still on. Excitement curled in his stomach. He forced it away, not wanting the emotion to distract him. If he couldn't guard her from the inside, he would from the outside. He felt like one of the detectives he read about all the time.

He settled back in the seat, scrunching down in a way that made him less visible to passersby, yet kept her door very visible to him. He couldn't do much about her back windows, he realized, then decided to patrol the rear of the building when he felt he'd be less likely to be seen. He worried about the lack of protection there in the meantime.

The cold fingers of the night breeze slowly wrapped around his ankles and legs as time wore on. Twinges of pain stiffened his neck. His butt began to hurt. Another growing problem reared its ugly little head.

He had to go to the bathroom.

Jared shifted in the car seat, trying to dispel all the discomforts plaguing him. He glanced at his watch. Fifteen minutes had passed since his return.

OK, he thought. So guard duty was slow going. He should have realized that.

Alison's lights went out.

OK, he thought again, this time with more enthusiasm. Now he was getting down to some serious guard duty.

Slowly, the dropping temperatures, cramped conditions and nature's call grew more uncomfortable. Only now they were overlaid by yet another problem. Exhaustion.

Tiredness threaded along his bones. His muscles weighed a ton. Even his head felt too big for his neck to keep upright. His eyes drifted shut a couple of times before he jerked fully awake. He rubbed his eyelids, trying to rub alertness back into his being. It didn't help. His only saving grace was that he was too damn cold and stiff to actually do more than doze momentarily.

Not to mention his other problem.

An endless hour after Alison's lights had gone off, he decided he could check the back without anyone's awareness. Most of the other lights in the building were out, too. He should be safe. And he could eliminate at least one problem he had.

Jared made a face at his own pun.

Glancing around to make sure he was alone, he opened his car door, got out and shut the door as quietly as he could, pleased with the slight snick of the lock catching. He glanced around again to ensure he'd not attracted attention. He hadn't. Nothing had changed from a moment ago.

Carefully, he picked his way across the sidewalk and grass, avoiding any small piles of leaves that had already fallen from the changing trees. *We'll have an early winter,* he acknowledged, then smiled at the incongruity of weather forecasting while on a secret mission to save a woman from her own folly.

He took advantage of a deeply shadowed tree and relieved one problem, then crept around the side of the building. He nearly fell into a stairwell leading to a basement. His stomach knotted anxiously when he realized the area wasn't well lit at all. Anyone could come here and—

"Freeze! Put your hands behind your head and get down on the ground on your stomach!"

Lights flashed around Jared, startling him and blinding him at the same time. He stared dumbly at them, blinking at their harshness.

"Hands up and get on your stomach!" someone shouted again.

Jared's brain kicked in. These were cops. "It's OK, Officer—"

"I *said* hands on your head and down on your stomach now!"

Jared realized explanations might not be appropriate at the moment. He laced his hands behind his head and dropped awkwardly to his knees. He wondered how to get the rest of the way down without falling flat on his face and decided it was impossible. He fell flat on his face as gently as he could. Damp, cold grass caressed his cheek. Wet seeped through his pant legs. *Wonderful,* he thought.

One of the police officers he had yet to see patted him down. "You have the right to remain silent—"

"Yes. I know," Jared began.

The cop continued, "If you give up that right, anything you say—"

"Officer, I know my Miranda rights. I'm an attorney." Jared's face heated. He hoped this never got out.

"Are you waiving your Miranda rights?"

"Yes. This is a simple mistake. Can I get up now?"

"No. You were spotted sitting in a car for over an hour by the citizens' watch group, then you came back here. Do you live in this complex?"

"No."

"Why are you behind this building?"

"I..." Jared realized that he could try to explain Alison's troubles, but she would deny them. He knew she would sound reasonable and he would sound like a stalker. By the time the entire thing was straightened out she would have vanished from his life. He couldn't allow that. "I lost something back here earlier this evening."

"What did you lose?"

"My house keys."

"I felt keys in your pocket. What were those?"

Jared flushed. "My house keys. See—"

"Why were you sitting in your car for so long if you thought you lost your keys back here?"

"I didn't want to disturb anyone."

"Uh-huh. Why didn't you check your pockets while you were in the car for an hour?"

Jared realized anything he said would only sound more stupid.

The cop obviously realized it, too, for he said, "Why don't we go to the station and straighten this out?"

Jared groaned.

Chapter Nine

Alison waited outside the police station, not knowing whether to laugh or yell. The object of her bemusement walked out into the early morning sunlight.

Humor won out.

She grinned at Jared's disheveled hair and clothes. His jawline was heavily shadowed with a new growth of beard. "My, my. We are getting downright adventurous, aren't we?"

"How did you know I was here?" he said, stopping next to her.

"I woke up for the last of the commotion and saw the police carting the 'perp' away. I put two and two together and figured out it was you. I can't wait to see the headlines: Attorney Caught Traipsing around in the Dark."

"There better not be any headlines," Jared said, his tone disgusted.

"In the famous words of Jay Leno," Alison said, "what the hell were you thinking?"

"I was thinking I was protecting you," he answered, looking away.

Alison burst into laughter. "Jared, I hate to be the

bearer of bad news, but you couldn't protect nectar from a butterfly.''

''Yeah, well…what are you doing here, anyway?''

''I bailed you out.''

He gaped at her. ''You did?''

''Someone had to. I thought you might need a ride back to your car and some breakfast. I'm cooking.''

''Thanks.''

She drove him back to the scene of his crime, her apartment building, in her little Fiero. He didn't say much in the car, subdued from his encounter with the other side of the law. She glanced over at him from time to time. At first she'd been appalled to hear of the trespasser last night from a neighbor. When everyone had gone outside to see what the excitement was about, she had spotted Jared's car and realized who the ''villain'' had to be. Her anger had shot to the fore, as she'd grasped the fact that he'd been spying on her. To protect her, no doubt. His performance in her apartment should have warned her. She should have known he'd given in too quickly.

But now she admitted he had been sweet to care that much about her. She couldn't remember anyone outside her immediate family who did. Unfortunately, she had no need of a knight in shining armor. Maybe last night's little fiasco would teach him to ride on to greener pastures. She wished he wouldn't, but knew it was for the best. She was only a dry, brown patch along the road.

He made a funny noise in the back of his throat when she eased her car into her designated parking slot.

''I must have been nuts,'' he said.

''I tried to tell you that last night,'' Alison couldn't help commenting. ''I was perfectly fine—''

"I meant about my methods. My reasons were sound."

"Your reasons were sweet, not sound."

He turned and grinned. "Sweet, eh?"

"Stop making an ass of yourself, and I'll make you something to eat if you like. I have cereal and toast and fruit galore."

"I'm there." He rubbed his stubble. "You got a razor? I feel like Mike Hammer after a three-day toot."

She chuckled at his old-fashioned slang. "I don't know. The grunge look is happening on you."

A few moments later, she let them both inside her apartment. "I wonder what the neighbors think, seeing me bringing in the big bad wolf on the morning after."

"They're probably thinking they could have saved themselves time and aggravation last night." He sat down at the kitchen card table. "What the hell is this citizens' group and where were they all night to spy on me like that?"

Alison put the kettle on for tea. "Joe, my neighbor who told me about the trespasser—namely you, although you weren't named at the time he told me—"

"Get on with it," he growled.

"Testy, aren't we?" she murmured, grinning. She couldn't help teasing him a bit. "Joe said they've had a citizens' watch group here for about two years, after a series of robberies at the apartments. They patrol regularly at night. You were lucky, sort of. The police had a bad accident to deal with on Route 95, otherwise they would have arrested you earlier."

"Good thing they didn't," he commented. "They would have gotten me on indecent exposure." He paused. "I had to go to the bathroom."

Alison burst into laughter.

"Speaking of that..." he said, raising eyebrows questioningly.

"Through the hallway and make a left. There's a package of razors in the medicine cabinet and a towel in the linen closet." Good thing she had done some emergency shopping for some linens on her first night at the apartment. At least she had a few towels. "You can help yourself to a bath if you like. And I hope you like, because you could probably use one."

"Thanks a lot."

He disappeared into the bathroom.

Still chuckling over his interesting evening, she got out cereal and fruit, bowls and utensils, in preparation for breakfast. She should have sent him on his way instead of asking him in, but she couldn't resist feeding him. He had got himself arrested in a misguided attempt to protect her. One had to feed a man who did that.

She heard the faint, low rumble of water being run in her tub. A fainter splash followed a few moments later. She realized that Jared was sitting in her bathtub—a naked Jared. Her heart beat faster and her skin warmed at the knowledge that a sexy man was in her home—such as it was—naked in her tub. Maybe the care and feeding of Jared Holiday wasn't such a good idea.

She tried to busy herself in order to block thoughts of Jared. Unfortunately, when cupboards were practically bare, one didn't have a thing to do.

He was just so sweet, she thought. Her resistance, never high around him, was nonexistent. She wanted so much to go in the bathroom and wash his back. In her mind's eye, she could see herself stripping away her clothes and joining him in the tub. Just a few steps and she could make her fantasy a reality. Later, she could watch him shave. She remembered being a little girl and watching her father shave. He had been a wonderful man and she missed him terribly. She had no doubt, however, that watching Jared shave would hold a whole new dimension for her.

She wondered what her life would have been like if her real father, a key witness to an underworld murder, hadn't been killed. Her mother wouldn't have been alone and pregnant. The woman had died a year after giving her daughter up for adoption. If all of that hadn't happened, Alison might have pursued her music rather than going into law enforcement. Maybe if all that hadn't happened and she had met Jared then, things would be different. Very different.

But they weren't.

She might not have met Jared, either. Certainly not her adoptive parents, wonderful people who had given her strong values. She had been lucky there. Life had, in the end, worked out for the best for her.

"Well, half the stink of prison is off me," Jared said, coming into the kitchen.

His hair gleamed wetly and his face was clean shaven. He still wore his clothes from yesterday, but he smelled of lilacs. Her soap...on his body.

Alison swallowed, suddenly very nervous. She pushed the emotions aside. "You were only in a holding cell and only for a few hours, hardly prison."

"You said I needed it."

"I said 'probably' and I said it just because you must be tired. A bath helps clear one's head."

"You know a lot of things, don't you?"

She grinned. "I try."

He sat down at the table again and pulled a bowl in front of him. "Hot dog! Cornflakes. My favorite. And an orange. You sure know how to reach a man's heart."

"If you're not careful, I might reach in and pluck it out."

"Isn't that Shakespeare or something? I don't suppose you have real coffee." He tapped the teapot, its contents now fully steeped.

"Convicts can't be choosers," she said, pouring him some tea.

"So I see." He grinned at her when she set the mug before him.

She sat down across from him and took the box of cornflakes, pouring some in her bowl.

"Food day, I see. Hey! Quit hogging the box!" He took it from her and poured himself some, then poured milk for both of them.

As they ate and crunched in a scene played out millions of times before by couples at the breakfast table, Alison tried not to think of the implications or the complications theirs had.

"I take it you don't like showers," he said finally, as the first rush of hunger was obviously satisfied.

She frowned, the comment puzzling her. "I like showers."

"You don't have a shower curtain, so I thought you were a bath fan."

She couldn't very well say she'd forgotten a shower curtain in her one-night frenzy to buy essentials for the apartment. "I wanted baths for a change."

She could see the questions in his eyes, and she thought about the bathroom and what it might have told him. Too much, with its nearly empty medicine cabinet and brand-new towels. He'd probably had to tear the price tag off one before he used it. She just hadn't been thinking when she'd made her offer. Why did her brain turn off so much around him?

Well, she had been avoiding a confrontation about last night. She'd better tackle the subject now.

"Jared, I hope you have learned your lesson," she said. "Trying to help when you don't know what you're doing only gets you into trouble."

"And we were having such a nice breakfast." He patted milk from his upper lip with his napkin.

"You're not going to do this again, are you?" she asked.

"I'm not?"

"Jared!" She glared at him, then sagged in defeat. "What am I going to do with you?"

"I can think of several things."

So could she. Alison propped her elbow on the table, then rested her chin in her turned up palm. She flipped back a straying hank of hair with her free hand. "Honestly, Jared. You have got to stop this protection nonsense. Last night was bad enough. You're lucky they're not pressing any charges, not even one for trespassing. I vouched for you, that you had been visiting me. Next time the police might not be so generous."

"I'll take my chances."

"Do you have a Good Samaritan complex?" she demanded, raising her head and glaring at him.

"Only with you."

He could make her crazy and endear himself to her in the same breath. He made her feel so good on a personal level: sexy and desired. He cared about her—even if he showed it in the strangest of ways. He'd said he loved her. While she considered him mixed-up emotionally, she still couldn't resist the lure that vow presented. Who could?

She didn't want to leave him, yet the time was nearly here for her to do so. Only how could she go without explaining the most vital bond that drew her to him? Couldn't she take something for herself for once? Couldn't she break the rules one time?

"You're looking at me funny," he said.

"Oh." She straightened.

"What were you thinking?"

She couldn't tell him. "Nothing."

He gave her a look that said he didn't believe her. "Let's try again. What were you thinking?"

She swallowed and admitted the truth. "About you."

He grinned, a too-pleased smile on his face.

"I was thinking you're a nut case."

"Oh."

She grinned back. "Finish your breakfast. Your orange is getting cold."

"OK."

He finished up as she ordered. Watching him, Alison's thoughts kept straying back to her earlier tempting ones. She tried to discipline them by mentally reciting the bureau policies on filing a report, but even that didn't help. She had only to look at his hair and want to ruffle it. His profile made Brad Pitt's look like Soupy Sales's. And Jared's mouth...watching him eat the orange was a study in voyeurism. When he sucked the juice out of a section before devouring it, she nearly fell out of the chair.

Lord help her, but she had it bad.

"I guess I better go," he said, finally getting to his feet. "I have a night's sleep to catch up on. With a citizen's watch here, you're more than OK."

Alison resisted the urge to say "My point exactly." *That* he wouldn't appreciate. She rose to her feet and walked him to the front door. "Thank you for trying to look after me last night. I appreciate the thought."

"But not the deed."

"Oh, no. I do. I just didn't need it." She chuckled, then sobered, remembering he probably didn't find his escapades nearly as funny as she did. She laid a hand on his arm, intending to bolster his bruised male-protector ego with some kindly words. Instead, the feel of his warm skin and the hard muscles underneath sent her senses spinning.

Even as she stretched on her toes to kiss him, she knew she shouldn't. But when her mouth touched his…when their tongues rubbed deliciously together, she forgot all her cautions. She only wanted all her longings to become reality.

Alison gripped Jared's arms, her fingers digging into his biceps as she pressed herself fully against him. He groaned, and she knew she'd surprised him. He wrapped his arms around her, his hands splaying across her back. His lips turned to pure fire, his tongue lapping at hers as if he desperately wanted to eat her up.

She loved it.

He spread hot, biting kisses over her cheeks and throat. She arched her neck back, giving him access. His hands knotted in her hair. His lips heated her sensitive skin. Heat penetrated every fiber of her being, rushed along her veins, pooled and throbbed intimately deep inside her. She dragged his mouth back to hers, kissing him almost wildly.

"If I don't go now, I'll never go," Jared whispered between scorching kisses.

She knew her answer before she said it, the only answer she could give. "Don't go."

Rules didn't matter a damn in the face of love.

HER WORDS BURNED through Jared as fast as her kisses had.

Her fingers worked open the buttons of his shirt and her palms spread across his chest. Her touch was like silk on his flesh, incongruously feminine and incredibly sensual. He couldn't think straight. He didn't want to. He only wanted her. He needed her. He had from the moment he saw her.

She pushed his shirt off him. It dropped to the floor.

"Your skin is so hot," she murmured, kissing his chest. Her lips were cool butterflies, sending his blood spiraling in his veins.

She was seducing him with her hands and mouth.

All his thoughts culminated in doing the same to her.

He lifted her off her feet and kissed her with hot, open-mouthed kisses. Holding her, he opened one eye and walked them into the bedroom, without breaking the kiss. The simple layout of the apartment didn't make the bedroom hard to find. Besides, he'd spotted it opposite the bathroom. The room had only a mattress and box spring. He pushed aside disturbing questions and decided she liked Japanese austerity in her decor. All he cared about was her and showing her how much he did.

"Oh, Lord, Jared," Alison moaned when they tumbled onto the mattress.

He chuckled at the extra-long fall, then pulled her sweater over her head. Her gorgeous strawberry blond hair spread out across her freckled shoulders. He reached behind her and fumbled with her bra before unhooking it. Pulling it from her, he freed her small breasts from their confines.

"You're beautiful," he said, his voice hoarse. "Perfect."

She looked up at him almost shyly, then he bent and

took one nipple in his mouth. It peaked against his tongue, hard and yet remarkably soft. Her hands clutched at his hair, pulling at it as her breathing quickened. He turned to the other nipple, as rosy as its twin, and sucked it to a diamond-hard point.

"Jared, please," she moaned.

She already pleased him beyond anything he could hope for. Her lips spread kisses in his hair. Her nails scratched at his back. She was a tigress already, and yet if she was gentle and submissive it wouldn't matter. Whatever made her Alison was all he needed.

They shed the rest of their clothes, fumbling and panting and laughing and helping each other. When Alison pushed her last sock off her foot, she suddenly threw herself across him, pushing him flat on the makeshift bed and straddling his waist. The most intimate part of her hovered just above him. If he went to his reward now, Jared thought, he'd die a happy man. She looked magnificent, like a Viking princess.

"Lower," he murmured, gazing in fascination at the light freckles that dusted her stomach and abdomen. They *did* go all the way down. He tried to push her farther down his own body and consummate his love for her.

Grinning slyly, she resisted. "You do the most wondrous things to me. Now it's my turn."

She kissed him at the corner of his mouth...his forehead...his chin...the other corner of his mouth....

Her breasts jiggled delightfully in front of his eyes. He tried to capture one with a kiss, but she was too quick for him, moving out of reach.

Her own kisses trailed lower, across his chest and stomach. She pressed herself more firmly against him, sliding backward in her effort to kiss every inch of skin.

Jared's world dimmed and he heard a moan of building pleasure. A full moment passed before he realized it was him making the sound. He caressed her thighs, loving the feminine strength in them.

Her kisses moved lower. *She* moved lower, tantalizing him with promised intimacy. Her hair spread out in a curtain across his stomach. He thought he would go insane as her hands and lips caressed his belly and thighs, never quite venturing further.

She was tormenting him beyond control. When he could stand it no longer, he pulled her upright with a growl, then rolled her over until he was on top of her. Her thighs cradled him.

She chuckled knowingly.

"You are a wicked woman," he said.

"I'm glad," she replied in a low voice, as she traced her fingers down the sides of his face.

He kissed her as she had him, not neglecting an inch of her flesh anywhere. She became a writhing, clawing thing beneath him, but still he wasn't satisfied. He needed this elusive woman who at turns exasperated and moved him. He needed to brand her with the essence of himself. He needed to bring her to his hand forever and let her fly at the same time.

"Jared, I want you," she moaned, bucking when he stroked her with gentle frenzy. "I *need* you."

He captured her mouth and sank into her until he was fully enveloped in her moist, satin depths. His brain and body spun wildly from the intimate bonding. He paused and gritted his teeth to keep control. From the first time he'd seen her, he had wanted this moment. He would not ruin it with a boyish reaction.

Slowly, he began to thrust into her, savoring the way their bodies met. She matched each thrust with one of her own, until they were moving faster and faster together. She wrapped her legs around his hips as the primitive rhythms of man and woman took them both deeper and higher. Their kisses burned hotter and hotter.

Alison stiffened and cried out, her pleasure triggering Jared's own. He thrust into her one last time, holding her tightly to him. His life force poured into her, and he let himself go, pulled into the velvet blackness with her. Never had he felt so complete. He had found the other half of himself; he had known it all along.

They lay together for endless minutes until Jared felt a trickle of wetness against his cheek. He was aware at the same time of Alison's hand on her face.

He raised his head. Her eyes were closed, yet tears leaked out of the sides of her eyelids.

"You're crying," he said, fascinated and shocked at her reaction to their lovemaking. "I was too rough, out of control. I'm so sorry, Alison—"

"No," she said, opening her eyes. "You were beautiful, too beautiful. Our lovemaking was beautiful...."

She burst into tears. Wrapping her arms around his neck, she buried her face in his shoulder and sobbed uncontrollably.

Bewildered, Jared tried to take heart from her clinging. If this had been his fault, she would have shot him by now. He held her tightly, kissing her hair and murmuring that everything was OK.

"I'm so sorry," she said finally, wiping her tears away with the back of her hand. "You must think I'm a nut."

"I think you're a lady who needs a good cry."

She laughed and hiccuped, holding back fresh tears. "Oh, Lord. I've saturated your shoulder."

She wiped at his wet flesh.

He took her hand and kissed her damp fingers, tasting the saltiness left from mingled weeping and lovemaking. "I'm not a suspicious man—"

Alison burst into laughter, her body shaking against his with her sudden amusement.

"But," he continued, "I have to ask why you need to cry. I hope I wasn't really that bad."

"I told you no, and I meant it." She kissed him, a tender kiss with much promise. "Our lovemaking was wonderful, all I could ask. I think you're right, though. I just needed a good cry."

He wished he could believe her, but he'd had too much evasiveness from her to do so. Her tears only reconfirmed that she was in trouble. Big Trouble. Their lovemaking had brought him much closer to her, but the thread could still snap. He knew she would have questions about his private life. He had questions about hers. No one in the nineties could afford to ignore them— even after the fact. But he would wait a little bit. They had more important matters to take care of.

He rolled her onto her back, taking her with him. They pushed the bedclothes down from underneath them, then pulled them up over themselves. Alison snuggled against him. Jared put his arm around her. He stroked her hair, marveling at how heavy it was as it flowed through his fingers. Her leg tangled with his, and he rubbed her foot with his own. Her hand played with his chest, slowly stroking paths through the short hairs and tickling his skin.

He was content to lay with her like this forever…never to ask questions, never to have the world intrude.

She rose up above him. "Jared, I wish I could tell you everything. I want to, but I can't."

That she admitted there was something to tell was huge progress.

"It's OK," he said. *For the moment.*

"I want to. I really do."

"OK." He sensed that any pressure would shut her down. Besides, he'd pressured her enough over the last few days. "I'll take you on faith, Alison."

"Good." She smiled tremulously.

He took her, again, with love.

JARED STOPPED AT HIS DESK in his study, groaning at the early Monday morning hour. Maybe staying the rest of the day and night at Alison's—and making love the rest of the day and night with her—had something to do with his fuzzy feeling. Maybe getting arrested had had a positive twist, after all, because he doubted he would have wound up at Alison's if he hadn't. He just hoped no one at the firm found out about his fiasco. After all, he was up for a partnership. Robert, being so fussy, wouldn't excuse misunderstandings. Right now, Jared better grab the work he'd neglected this weekend and get to the office.

As he riffled through the center desk drawer, his list of perfect attributes in a wife caught his eye. He drew it out, feeling as if Alison must match up with a few more of them now.

IDEAL-MATE ATTRIBUTES
by Jared Holiday

I. Physical Beauty

    A. Dark hair, straight; preferably sophisticated style

    B. Doelike brown eyes

C. Exotic features, delicate

D. Creamy skin, absolutely unblemished

E. Large breasts

F. Small waist

G. Long, slender legs

H. Petite frame, but negotiable as long as it looks good

I. Two years younger than husband (me)

OK, he thought, and crossed out the whole section. Alison was Alison—positively gorgeous, especially naked—and he couldn't ask for more.

II. Intelligence

A. MBA, at least

B. Attended Ivy League school

C. Have had at least one scholarship for grade-point average

D. Shrewd in personal finances

E. Can assess people and situations quickly

He'd crossed out *A* and *B* before. Instead, he decided to change *A* to "Have educational background," *B* to "Is skilled at her work" and *C* to "Passed the fifth grade." He figured fifth grade was a sure bet. He could change *D* to... He crossed out *D* altogether. He had enough money for both of them. *E* could stay. She was very good at that.

III. Personal Background

A. Personal wealth preferable, enough to live comfortably

    B. Parents, relatives have personal wealth/no
       bums
    C. Family name of some social standing
    D. Race unimportant, but prefer Asian

He hadn't touched this section before but had thought
about axing it. He made a big black X over the whole
section.

"Works for me," he said, grinning.

IV. Career

    A. Well along her corporate ladder
    B. Has a commitment to her job
    C. Totally understands his needs with his job
    D. Does not plan to interrupt career for family

"Hell," he muttered, feeling like he ought to rewrite
this entire section, too. Either it didn't fit Alison or he
didn't feel the need for these things anymore.

V. Social Abilities

    A. Adapts to any situation
    B. Can talk with anybody about anything knowl-
       edgeably
    C. Thrives on social situations
    D. Loves to entertain; last-minute guests are
       never a problem
    E. Understands the importance of entertaining for
       husband's career
    F. Will further her husband's cause in any way
       she can
    G. Is active in at least two community organi-
       zations

He felt better about *A*, *B* and *C*. She did take things in stride, so maybe *D* would be OK, except he thought the last part of *D* would be rather inconsiderate of him. Maybe *E* was OK. Maybe not. He crossed it out. On *F* he added the caveat that it would be legal and ethical. On *G* he changed it to whatever she wanted to involve herself in. That was fine with him.

VI. Personal Likes and Dislikes

    A. Takes great care of her person; always looks perfect day and night

    B. Is a tigress in bed

    C. Defers to husband's opinions, career and needs above her own

    D. Wants two children and will be very giving mother to them

    E. Likes nouvelle cuisine—cooks like a pro

    F. Likes plays

    G. Likes symphonies

    H. Likes foreign films over domestic

    I. Dresses in designer clothes, European flair

    J. Likes jazz over other types of music

    K. Generally very upscale in her total outlook

    L. Calm nature; prefers smoothing matters over to fighting

Jared groaned again, reading this section. Hell, even he didn't like foreign films or jazz music. He'd been a real preppie then. He moved *B* to the *A* spot and starred it. He was no fool. He checked *A* because she always looked wonderful. He tossed *C*; her opinion mattered very much to him. He thought *D* was great, and *E* didn't matter a damn, so he crossed it out. *F* and *G* were OK, he hoped she liked them, too. He changed *I* to "Whatever makes her happy." *K* got stroked out. *L...* He decided to let it stay. Better she would want to smooth things over than take her gun to him. He would have to do something about that gun—like take it and hide it.

VII. Most Important

    A. Love is not a requisite for her for marriage

    B. She sees the value of good companionship and sharing similar interests with her husband.

    C. Although not a proponent of open marriage for herself, she will turn an occasional blind eye to her husband's outside needs.

Jared made a face and took out *A* and *C*. *C!* He would kill her if she did a *C* to him. He wanted no other man to know her like he did. He wasn't even happy that they had pasts not involving each other, but life couldn't be helped. He added a new one to the list: Honesty. He wanted that above all.

Note: Candidates must reach 75% of attributes for serious consideration.

Jared stared at the revised figure of seventy-five percent. Still too high. He changed it to fifty percent.

"All right!" he exclaimed, pleased with himself. And with Alison.

Chapter Ten

Alison tried to concentrate on the file she had to micro-film. She'd made it halfway down one huge row of files since being put on this job, and she was proud of that. But it would take forever to finish.

She didn't have forever. She had barely any time left. With Jared.

Alison curled her fingers around the hard metal of the machine. She had thrown all her walls down and followed her heart. She did not regret the decision, no matter how impulsive it had been. But now she didn't want to leave. Yet she knew she had to. Jared wouldn't accept her deceptions—not when he was convinced she was in danger. He would be humiliated if he knew the truth.

"Why couldn't he be a creep?" she murmured in disgust. "Then he wouldn't be trying to save me."

Unfortunately, this job gave her too much time to think when she only wanted to feel. She wanted Jared back in her bed. They hadn't gotten out of it until this morning—except to pay the pizza-delivery man. She wanted to be in Jared's bed, too. She wanted to continue to break every rule and tell him everything.

She nearly had.

He deserved the truth. That was part of why she had

cried after making love with him—that and knowing she would have to leave him soon. She couldn't tell him, and not just because of the lie. Her need for justice was too strong. Her need to live secretively was too ingrained. She had a job she couldn't give up, not without people being hurt in some way if she did. She had cried, too, for what she couldn't have—a true relationship with him. She had cried because she took more than she gave to him.

E.J. came into the microfilm room, her expression distraught. "I hate this place."

Alison looked up at her. "Having a bad day, I take it."

"I'm sorry to bother you. I usually come in here to vent because it's empty most of the time."

"What's the problem?"

"It's not mine. It's Jared's."

Alison felt as if some unseen fist had just punched her in the gut. "What's wrong? Is it me?"

E.J. stared at her. "Why would it be you?"

Obviously their lovemaking was still a secret. Alison cleared her throat. "I thought maybe I did something wrong when I worked for him."

"No, not unless you wiped out his last quarter's billings from the face of the earth. They're missing. He swears he gave the list to accounting weeks ago, but accounting says they've never seen it. Now he can't even find the disk file. That bastard accounting manager waited until the partners' meeting this morning to announce it. He never said a word to Jared before this." Her tone turned sarcastic. "He didn't feel he had to...." She paused. "Robert pitched a fit in front of everyone about Jared being careless."

Alison's heart dropped. She wished she'd been with

him this morning. Maybe she could have helped some-how. She felt helpless as it was. "Could Jared's new secretary have it? Didn't she type it up?"

"No. The attorneys have to do it themselves. Robert insists on that for confidentiality. I wish I knew what happened to it." E.J. leaned forward. "I should be neu-tral, but I want Jared to get the partnership. We need someone like him to balance Robert. Margaret's just as acerbic as Robert, Mark's too lazy and Bill's weak, too conciliatory."

Alison wanted Jared to get the job because she cared so much about him. She wanted him to succeed in ev-erything he wanted. "What can I do to help?"

"Nothing, unfortunately."

"Can it be built back up?"

"It has to be. Jared's in his office, trying now. He's got to do it out of his head, if he can't find it, but even his file notes are missing. What a mess!"

"Poor Jared," Alison murmured. Her stomach churned. She hated the thought of him being in trouble.

E.J. left a few minutes later, and Alison slipped out of the file room. She hurried down to Jared's office. His secretary was away from her desk. Alison smiled grate-fully that she didn't have to run the gauntlet of awkward questions and requests. She knocked on his closed door.

"What!" he snapped from inside, clearly angry at be-ing disturbed.

Alison swallowed, wondering if it would have been better to leave him alone. Unfortunately, she was com-mitted. She opened the door and poked her head in.

"Hi. I hear you're having a problem. Can I help?"

"Dammit! Did *everyone* hear Robert dress me down like a two-year-old?" He ran his hand through his hair in frustration.

"Maybe I better come back later," Alison began.

"No." His anger deflated and he looked lost. "No. Come in. I need a hug."

She walked in and closed the door behind her. "I have a big one for you."

She went to him and put her arms around his shoulders. She kissed his temple.

He sighed. "I feel better and yet I don't."

"If it helps, I don't think it's all over the office. E.J. vented in the file room, a place she considers private. She forgot about me until it was too late, I guess. She's ticked off."

"If E.J. knows then it's all over the office." Jared squeezed Alison's forearm, then patted it. "Thanks for trying, though."

She let go of him; he seemed to want that. "Can I help you in any way?"

He smiled wryly. "I can think of one, but it would probably get me in more trouble."

Her too, she acknowledged, the word *trouble* reminding her of yesterday's unprotected sex. She had risked more than her job and her integrity for him. At least they'd talked about their past experiences and knew they were both physically healthy.

"Is the missing stuff like that billing I did when I temped for you?" she asked, knowing she shouldn't take his time unless she made it profitable.

"No, this is an item-by-item accounting we have to keep internally. Our end-of-year bonuses and the partners' profit sharings are based on them. You screw them up and you're dead meat." He made a face. "I'm dead meat."

"Isn't that like keeping a second set of books?"

"Not really. We charge the clients by the firm's

hourly rate. Billable hours are calculated in actual costs, plus there's other information that goes into the quarterly version that the attorneys have to prepare.''

She wandered around to the front of his desk. She fiddled with the Justice statue, then picked it up. As she held the figure, a funny feeling of déjà vu came over her, as if she'd seen the billing. Yet how could she have, when Jared himself said she hadn't? ''Are you sure it isn't what I saw?''

''I wish it were.'' He stared at his computer screen. ''Dammit. I have got to find those files. I can't rebuild it all from memory. It's three months' work. My files ought to be here, even if they were corrupted somehow. Or the entire drive ought to be wiped out.''

''That's the way I understand these things work.'' Alison knew a fair amount about computers. Some viruses or corruptions of files would scramble or eliminate everything in the computer's storage area. Other computer viruses only scrambled the data within a file, but would leave the file name intact—a sneakier corruption because the operator didn't know anything was wrong until he or she actually opened the file. Viruses didn't pick and choose their victims, especially something specific like billing files, while leaving everything else alone. That was a little too smart for a virus. Most virus makers aimed at wholesale destruction.

''Could you have accidentally wiped out your billing files?'' she asked.

''I kept them in their own subdirectory. I would have had to wipe that out, too, because it isn't here, either. I couldn't have done it without going into another program altogether. Or I would have had to kill the files one by one. I know that much.'' He sank down in the chair, resting his head on the tall back in a gesture of defeat. "There were over forty files. Maybe more."

Alison wasn't about to let him go down without a fight. "Do you keep a backup on a tape drive?"

He snorted in clear disgust. "I have a tape-drive backup but it's a pain in the ass to use, so I never remember to do it. I think I've learned a lesson I didn't want to know."

"Yes, you have," she agreed firmly.

He glared at her. "Good thing you turn me on, otherwise I'd be strangling you at the moment."

"I'm always pleased to help," she said, grinning. She thought a moment. "Do you have a utility program on your machine? If you haven't saved anything since the files disappeared, we might be able to resurrect them. They'll just be sitting there hidden—provided nothing new has been written over top of them. A blank page isn't quite a blank page with computers."

"How do you know that?" he asked.

Another foot in mouth, she thought. "I have to use computers, so I figured it was best to know how to keep myself out of trouble. You got a problem with that, Mr. Inquisitor?"

He sat up, looking hopeful again. "Not me. I love you for it, and I do have a utility program, but I only know how to use it to manage the files. You know, adding and deleting." He slumped. "Wait. No good. I saved something earlier, when I was working on notes for a trial tomorrow."

"If nothing else, the utility will tell you if other files are corrupted and what kind of virus got in your machine. Were you on the Internet recently, or did you use a friend or co-worker's diskette? That could have put the corruption there."

"No, I haven't." He fiddled with the computer, finding the utility program. That he had one, and even better, a popular one that she knew how to work, gratified Alison.

"OK, set it to scanning your drive," she said.

"Right." By his hesitation she knew he hadn't done it before. She came around his desk and put her hand over his on the mouse. His fingers were strong and warm, just as they had been on her body. She guided their hands together to the proper commands, and the screen began flipping to the proper sequences for scanning.

"That should do it," she said, smiling at him.

"Thank you." He lifted her fingers to his lips and kissed the back of her hand.

His door opened at the same moment. Robert stood on the threshold. "Jared..."

The man paused, gaping, as the scene before him registered.

Alison muttered a barnyard curse and slipped her hand from Jared's. In her best business voice, she added, "When the scan is finished, you'll know whether the files are still there or whether they're corrupted completely."

"Chicken," Jared muttered, right before she made her escape.

She avoided Robert's sour gaze and was careful not to touch him as she passed by on her way out of Jared's office. *Poor Jared,* she thought, feeling guilty for leaving him to Robert. This just wasn't his day.

When she finally sat back down at her desk in the file room, a twin sense of urgency and familiarity overwhelmed her.

"Why do I keep thinking I've seen his files?" she

murmured to herself. He'd said she hadn't. Maybe she felt that way because she cared so much about him. She shouldn't, but it was far too late.

She set the nagging thought aside and began microfilming older files. The worked bored her to tears, depressed her with its drudgery and killed her back from having to hunch over the machine.

She loved it—but only because it kept her near Jared.

Some of the files from years ago boggled her mind. The crazy lawsuits filed, the nuts whose interviews read like a Marx brothers movie, the incredible amount of money that had poured into the firm back then... No wonder Robert was so fastidious about the billing. She would be, too, if she were him.

Alison straightened away from the machine, feeling as though someone had just punched her in the stomach. No wonder she felt as though she'd seen the billing Jared had described to her. She had, in a way, with the older versions she was converting.

The file In basket caught her eye. Something clicked in her head. She went over to the basket, hoping her crazy, long-shot notion was valid. She came up empty after flipping through the basket's contents, most of it being from the last few working days. Glancing around the "miles of files," she wondered if Jared's stuff had already been filed.

She walked down the aisles, tracing her fingers along the rows until she came to his recent files. She pulled the first big folder and glanced inside. Nothing. In fact, his files contained no billings at all. She went to the accounting section, then looked furtively around the room. She really shouldn't go into these files, she thought, knowing they were very confidential. She wasn't working in the recent files—and probably wouldn't for a long time. She ought to ask E.J. to look for her.

To hell with it, she decided. This was for Jared.

Right at the beginning of the file for the last quarter was the paperwork she'd noted a few weeks earlier in the In basket. Jared's paperwork. The detailed spreadsheet left no doubt she was looking at what had caused this morning's hoopla at the partners' meeting. She flipped through every page, just to be sure of the dates involved. She definitely had the right file.

Heart beating happily, Alison pulled out the paperwork and nearly ran from the room in her haste to get it to Jared. She rushed past the big copy machine, then skidded to a halt. Setting the billing sheets on the automatic tray changer, she made four copies of Jared's quarterly billing.

"Just to be safe," she told the wall, while listening to the *shoop, shoop, shoop* of the machine sucking in and spitting out each page.

She got Jared's secretary, now at her desk, to buzz her in. The woman gave her a strange look, but Alison didn't care.

"I was just about to get you," Jared said. He tapped his monitor screen. "How long will this scan take?"

"I don't know. An hour, maybe more. Jared—"

"An hour!" He cursed enough to make a dockworker proud. "Robert wants me to redo the file by five tonight, and he made it clear my partnership candidacy is on the line. Stop the damn program now!"

"No need." She grinned and held up the papers in her hand. "I found it."

His jaw dropped. "What?"

"I found your quarterly billing in the file room," she said.

He nearly jumped out of his chair and scrambled over to her. He yanked the paperwork from her hands, then immediately said, "It can't be. It's too thick."

"I made four copies," she said smugly. "In case it gets lost again. Read it, you dingdong."

He gazed at the first page, then said with growing excitement, "This is it...this is it!"

He grabbed her and spun her around, kissing her soundly. The papers fell to the floor when he kissed her again, with more passion than gratitude.

"You are the most marvelous creature," he said, leaning his forehead against hers. "Have I told you that before?"

"Not nearly enough." She giggled, happy she had helped him. "I'm so pleased for you, Jared."

He kissed her again, his tongue mating intimately with hers. "I'm so happy to have you. How did you find this, Alison? Where did you find it?"

"In the file room." She lowered her voice. "Don't tell anyone, but I looked in the accounting files."

"My lips are sealed...mostly by yours."

She chuckled. "I kept thinking I'd seen what you described, and when I was microfilming an old billing file, it clicked that I had seen it in the to-be-filed basket a few weeks ago. At least it was worth a look. And I found it."

"Lunch and dinner and every meal after that is on me," Jared vowed. "After I shove this billing under Robert's nose and scream about accounting's mismanagement. I'll be nice about it." He grinned. "But not *that* nice."

"I should hope not." She grinned in return. "I was a bad girl going into those files."

He kissed her under her ear, starting the most delicious tingle running down her body. "You are very bad. I love it."

She wanted to say the words back to him. She couldn't, knowing she would have to tell him the truth at some point and he would probably hate her. But how she wanted to.

Eventually, they picked up the papers from the floor. Alison promised to put the copies on his desk while he shoved the originals in everyone's face. She sent him off to the office wars with one last kiss.

After he left on his mission, she set the copies on his desk. Glancing at the monitor screen, she was pleased to see the scan was about one-third of the way done. So far it looked clean, showing no errors.

Well, it had a long way to go, she acknowledged, then remembered today was a fruit-and-veggie day for her.

"Oh, to hell with it," she murmured, smiling.

Today deserved a feast.

JARED TOOK HER to the supermarket after work that night.

Alison stood in the produce section, frowned and said, "What's this?"

He laughed. "Dinner. Take your pick."

"But you took me to a supermarket for lunch today."

"Dinner's on me, too."

She put her arm around his shoulders and walked him past the broccoli and peppers. "Jared, honey, you are cooking me a dinner with loads of meat and fat, OK? It's going to cost you a fortune, understand? I saved your butt, and a cute butt it is—"

"Thank you." He broke in, kissing her cheek and loving her playfulness.

"You're welcome. Now I want my reward. You promised. You deliver."

"I should have promised sex," he whispered in her ear, not caring about the other shoppers around them. "I'd love to deliver that."

"You deliver dinner, and I'll deliver dessert," she whispered back.

"Hot dog."

She led him down aisles, her arm through his, their hips bumping together familiarly as they wove around the other shoppers. Alison's face glowed with amusement and determination. Jared grinned, never more pleased in his life than to be with her and see her happy. Her emotions fed his soul.

She picked two strip steaks from the butcher's department, along with scalloped potatoes and apple rings from Ready-To-Eat. The upscale market had all kinds of fresh vegetable dishes at which she turned up her nose.

"We're eating fat and hearty tonight," Alison announced.

Jared chuckled. "Damn. My computer ought to eat my files more often."

They drove separately to his house, where he broiled the steaks and reheated the potatoes and vegetables. They sat in the kitchen to eat.

"I wish I had a picture to show you of Robert's face when I handed him the billing," Jared said wistfully as they ate in the kitchen. "It was priceless."

"You should have heard him in accounting afterward. He ripped into Drew, the manager, about losing your file and causing all kinds of grief," Alison said. She took a bite of dinner, then added, "Boy, this is good."

"Almost as good as what I could make," Jared admitted.

"It's as good as I could buy."

He grinned. "True. What a great day out of disaster."

"I'm still bothered by what happened to the files on your computer," Alison said, frowning. "I thought the scan would come up with a bunch of errors, not the small amount it did. And the errors were nothing to speak of, either, just normal blips with opens and closures that happen naturally over the life of a disk drive."

The scan had shown no viruses or corruptions. Unfortunately, the billing files couldn't be resurrected. They must have been missing long enough for Jared to have saved another file that overwrote the billing directory. He hadn't noticed their absence. He'd had no need to go into the billing directory recently, and he just hadn't paid attention to it. He never paid attention to files he wasn't currently using. Who would? From now on he would, though. He'd learned his lesson and didn't want to see another incident like this one again.

"Maybe I better have someone in to look over my computer," he said. "Something might be going wrong with it, even though I haven't noticed anything. I don't want to lose any other files."

"Good thought. I'd love to know exactly what happened, though. I'm no expert with computers, but I know that sort of corruption isn't usual. Maybe you picked up some kind of weird new virus."

He was less bothered by the computer problem than she was. Hell, he was only glad for the solution she'd provided. "Why do I feel like the Center for Disease Control will be all over me?"

She laughed. "Because you're very cute."

He smiled. "I am?"

"Of course you are, and you know it. Ah...did Robert

say anything about your kissing my hand? I've been afraid to ask.''

"Not a word." Jared picked up her hand and kissed it again, just for luck. "I think he was completely thrown by my finding the file."

"That's an odd reaction on his part," she commented, after he let her hand go. "I would think he'd just be happy that the information was found."

"Robert's unique unto himself," Jared said. "He's not a totally bad guy, just a very fussy one."

"I've seen that a lot with the temp jobs I've worked," Alison commented. "It's a little amazing that fussy people are given top-management jobs where they alienate the people who work for them, a lot of times enough so that they can't keep anybody for a long period. I worked at a property-management place and the head of that subdivision had been through fourteen office managers in less than a year."

"Sounds like Robert's soul mate," Jared said.

"That guy needed an E.J. to handle him," Alison added.

"So why didn't you take the job?" Jared asked. "I know you well enough to know that you can handle a Robert type as easily as E.J."

She shuddered. "No, thanks. No job is worth the aggravation."

He knew it was more than that. She wasn't afraid of aggravation or confrontation. Her evasiveness had a more sinister source. He had managed, through the arrest and its aftermath, to keep her occupied for two nights since he'd discovered her gun. After making love to her, it was more imperative than ever that he free her from her threat. He loved her, had loved her at first sight. She wouldn't commit to him until she was free of her past—whatever that was.

"As long as Robert doesn't find out about my little brush with the law, I'm OK."

She smiled. "He won't. I promise not to tell."

"If you tell, I'll be sitting in your other lawn chair. Speaking of lawn chairs, when are you getting the stuff for my house?"

"You never give up, do you?"

"Nope. So when?"

"This week, I guess. I still can't figure out what you want."

"Whatever *you* want," he said, and meant it.

She looked heavenward, as if for help.

After dinner, while they cleaned up, he said, "By the way, when's dessert? You promised."

She straightened from the dishwasher. "So I did." She thrust a dirty plate into his hands. "Here, you finish, then come upstairs. And wash your hands before you do."

"Yes, ma'am," he said meekly, as she disappeared from the kitchen.

He couldn't wait to find out why he needed clean hands, and he finished loading the dishwasher in record time. Whatever questions he had about her past—and their future—went out of his head as he climbed the stairs. He went into his room.

She lay naked on his black coverlet.

Jared sucked in his breath, his physical reaction already having him near to bursting. Her body was like soft cream against the dark silk. Her rosy nipples pouted for attention. Her hair was spread out across the pillows like a satin fan. She had a little, triumphantly feminine half smile on her lips. Jared suddenly understood Mona

Lisa's look. That fine lady had been seducing Da Vinci during the painting of her portrait—and doing a damn good job of it, if Da Vinci had been any kind of man at all.

"I love dessert," he said hoarsely, approaching the bed.

"I hoped you might. This has been a little fantasy of mine ever since I saw your bed."

"Fantasize no further." He stripped off his clothes, fumbling with buttons, pants and socks. Alison watched him the entire time. He hoped he matched all her fantasies about him. She stretched. He nearly fell over his own two feet.

After he shed his briefs, he leaped onto the bed in his eagerness. Alison giggled.

"Lord, but you make me feel like it's my first time again," he murmured, pulling her to him.

She pressed against his body, her naked flesh more delicious than any dessert could ever be. "This is our first time in your bed."

"But not the last," he vowed.

He kissed her.

SOMETHING PENETRATED his sleep. Jared opened his eyes to darkness, yet he sensed dawn wasn't far away. He heard a piano being played somewhere in his house at the same time he recognized Alison was no longer in his bed. He got up and found a robe, then put it on and went downstairs.

Alison sat at the baby grand, gently playing a Chopin nocturne. She wore her shirt, but he didn't know if she was fully dressed, since he could only see her shoulders. He didn't turn on the light. Enough came from the street to enable him to make her out well enough in the shadows.

The baby grand was more for show nowadays, his thirst for lessons five years ago having long ago panned out. She played with experience, although she stumbled over passages as if she was rusty. She probably was.

Spotting him finally, she stopped and said, "I woke you. I'm sorry. I couldn't resist playing. It's been years."

He felt her vulnerability, a wall seemingly breached. "Where did you learn to play?"

"As a kid." She chuckled. "Didn't we all? I played clarinet, too, in my high-school band."

"You play very well."

"I'm too out of practice, but this nocturne was my father's favorite, so I must have played it a thousand times since I was twelve. It's like riding a bicycle. You never quite forget."

"What else haven't you forgotten?" he asked, coming to her. To his relief, she was only in her shirt, clearly indicating she had no plans to leave him. Yet.

"What do you mean?" she asked, her voice wary.

"Nothing." He was walking on eggshells as it was, and he knew it. "Stay with me."

"I can't stay," she said, playing riffs and measures of songs. "I've got to get ready for work in a few hours."

"I'm not talking about tonight."

Her fingers froze over the keys, the music stopping abruptly. "I can't stay, Jared."

"Yes, you can," he said, deliberately not touching her. "I'll protect you. I have resources—"

She reached out and put a finger to his lips. "Don't ruin it. Please don't ruin it."

He sighed, then kissed her finger. "For now. But I'll ask you again. Soon."

She nodded and went back to her playing.

He wanted so much to ask her if she loved him. He needed to hear the words just once. She had to say them soon, he thought.

She had to.

JARED ENTERED the small studio, amazed how cramped his cousin's working conditions were—as amazed as he was each time he visited Raymond here. The On Air light was dark, so Jared knew it was OK to invade. Besides, Raymond's radio sports-talk morning show had been over for two hours.

His cousin was fiddling with some dials and holding a headset up to one ear. Suddenly, he threw the headset down on the floor. "This stuff never works!"

"It might if you didn't throw it, Ray," a disembodied feminine voice advised him.

"Technicalities," Raymond said, then grinned at Jared. He shook his cousin's hand. "Hey, Mr. Attorney. Nice surprise."

"I thought I'd take you to lunch...if you're finished abusing the equipment."

"The headset went out on me halfway through the show." Raymond snorted. He flipped on a switch, then said into a microphone, "It's this cheap stuff we buy."

"Become number one in the morning-drive arbitrons and then we'll talk," said the disembodied voice. "Hi, Jared."

"Hi, Karen," Jared called out. He had met Raymond's long-suffering producer on several occasions.

"I'm number six in the ratings, and that's coming off a miserable baseball season. A miracle of radio talent if

I say so myself, yet she has the nerve to complain,'' Raymond said, making a face. ''Hell, man. Let's go to lunch.''

They picked a little bistro in Philadelphia's Center City, not far from Raymond's building. Jared had eaten here before with Raymond and was undaunted by the lunchtime crowd, knowing the traffic moved in and out quickly.

As they sat at a small round table, Jared admitted that Raymond might not be the best person to talk to about woman troubles. His cousin, an on-air flirt, was an off-air misogynist. To Jared's knowledge, Ray rarely dated; he claimed he had no time for socializing. But Peter and Michael, having just married, had no women problems. They'd be looking with rose-colored glasses on relationships and wouldn't understand Jared's difficulties with Alison. Raymond would at least have a less-biased prospective. Jared hoped.

After they got their meal and talked about life in general, Jared finally told Raymond about Alison and his concerns. He didn't leave a thing out, not even his arrest.

Raymond finally sobered, after laughing at Jared's little jailhouse adventure. ''You fell in lust, kid. And you said ages ago that there was no such thing as love at first sight. Does no one in this family listen to himself anymore?''

''Ray, I know lust. This was more, right from the first. But what do I do about the trouble she's in?''

''I knew you'd walked off the edge of the plank when you brought her to Michael's. With those hawks, Mary Ellen and Janice, hovering to get us, that should hardly inspire bringing a casual date. They were all over Alison like white on rice.''

''I like Mary Ellen and Janice,'' Jared said.

"Did I say I didn't?" Raymond asked, his tone aggrieved. "I did not. I think they're great. Peter and Michael are happy, but you've got to keep your head, man, about Alison. You've got to keep your head about women as a whole." Raymond waved his fork to emphasize his point. "Jared, women are manipulators. They know exactly how to work a man to make him crazy. They flirt. They put on this kind of come-hither persona and when we come hither, they push us away. When we're in a frenzy from chasing them, they reel us in like the great flopping fish we are. Years later, when we wake up from our stupor, they've got the house, the car, the dog, the kids and the checkbook. We've got our manhood in the gutter. And that's only if we're lucky."

"Some girl must have really hurt you," Jared said.

"Naa." Raymond chuckled. "Hell, I've just kept my eyes open, and that's given me some objectivity on the subject. Look at how elusive Alison's been. She's got you strung along like you're a june bug in a little kid's clutches. She's not falling all over you, trying to get your attention. Instead, she's exploited all your male instincts to hunt, until she's hooked you good."

"No. She's in trouble, Ray. I've helped too many women not to know the signs."

"Jared, old son, you have always had a white-knight complex…and you make a ton at it, too. That's fine. But Alison's tapped into that. Oh, I grant you, she's striking, with that hair, and she's quiet and congenial. At least she was that way at Michael's. Call her bluff."

"What the hell are you talking about?" Jared demanded. He must have been nuts to think Raymond had an insight to help him with Alison.

"Call her bluff," Raymond repeated. "Do a background check on her. You shark lawyers have your detectives on retainer. Use one of them to get the essentials on Alison. If she is in trouble, then you ought to know, and I'll be the first to say mea culpa. And if she's not, then you know she's been playing an elaborate game to get your interest *up*."

"It's up all right," Jared muttered, understanding Raymond's drift all too well.

"There you go. Get a little downside happening, and you'll be better off. You'll be thinking straight again, too."

Jared wasn't so sure about that. "Maybe she's been hurt by some man, and she's just being emotionally cautious."

"Keep believing that, and I've got a bridge to sell you," Raymond said.

"I'd love to see you turned upside down by a woman," Jared told his smug cousin. "You would be a wreck."

"It ain't gonna happen in your lifetime, pal," Raymond replied confidently. "I'm immune to women. I discovered that years ago."

So far Raymond *had* been immune. Jared supposed his cousin was right about some women. But he wasn't right about Alison.

He couldn't be.

Chapter Eleven

"What happened with Jared?"

Alison stared at E.J., who had come into the microfilm room and dropped a bombshell. Alison assumed it was a bombshell. She decided to play dumb and ask first. "What do you mean, what happened with Jared? Did he lose another billing file?"

There, she thought. *Now that sounded innocent.*

"Not that I know of. Robert came to me this morning and said something about Jared kissing you last week." E.J. grinned. "So spill the beans. I knew Jared was attracted to you. He doesn't let just anyone decorate his office."

Oh boy, Alison thought. It was the bombshell. She shrugged. "There's nothing to it. I showed him how to scan his computer for corruption and viruses the day he lost his files. I hoped we could find them on the disk drive, although hidden somehow. We didn't. But he kissed my hand when he thought there was a chance we would. Robert came in the moment he did. See? Nothing to it."

"Good thing Robert didn't walk in after you found the original files. I bet he would have discovered you sprawled across Jared's desk in a thank-you to end all thank-yous.''

"E.J.!" Alison blushed tomato red. She could feel the heat in her cheeks. "You *know* Jared never did such a thing on his desk.''

"Maybe not his desk, but you're not blushing for nothing. What's going on with you two?" E.J. leaned forward. "Don't worry about Robert. I told him you were grown-ups and to mind his own business. Besides, he was a little late to be moaning about it now. He's ticked at me, but someone's got to tell him to butt out occasionally. We don't have a policy on office dating, but even if we did, you'd be exempt because you're employed by someone else and do contract work for us.''

"E.J., there's nothing between Jared and me." Alison held up her hand in a pledge. "I swear.''

She hadn't lied. When she and Jared were together, nothing *was* between them, not even clothes.

"How gullible do you take me for?" E.J. demanded.

"Very?" Alison asked.

"Try again. So, girl, spill your guts.''

Everybody was in the act now, Alison thought. "There's nothing to spill.''

When she added no further comment and the silence stretched out, E.J. eventually got the message that Alison wasn't talking. "All right, don't spill. But I'll worm everything out of you. I'm very good at that.''

"Wonderful," Alison muttered, thinking Art would kill her for having yet another bloodhound on her trail. What the heck was she doing to have all this interest in her? "Is Robert going to fire me over this?''

"No." E.J. chuckled. "I do the office hiring and firing, and I have plenty of reasons to keep you on.''

Relieved, Alison said, "Good. I've never been asked to leave a temp job or been taken out of one, either, so I'd like to keep my record spotless. Robert seeing that little kiss on my hand won't affect Jared's chances for the partnership job, will it?"

That was her biggest fear.

"With Robert that's hard to say." E.J. leaned forward again and added in a low voice, "Robert's always been a little jealous of Jared. Jared's the most profitable attorney, and he's congenial with the staff, something Robert's not. If Jared doesn't get the partnership, that'll be the reason more than anything else."

"But that's not fair!" Alison exclaimed.

Robert's secretary came into the file room. E.J. smiled at the woman, then gave Alison a raised-eyebrowed look. "Be sure and microfilm the individual files in chronological order for that year."

"Do you want them separated by years or do you want a subject file to hold all the material currently in the archives?" Alison asked, knowing they were putting on a show for Robert's secretary. This was a late date to be getting these instructions, but the secretary didn't know that.

"What do you think?" E.J. asked.

"Is that a rhetorical question or a request for an opinion?"

E.J. laughed. The secretary did, too.

"A request," E.J. said.

"Keep them separated by years," Alison said promptly, since that was what she'd been doing—per E.J.'s original instructions. "I think that's how people would expect them to be done and will try to find them."

"OK."

The secretary left.

"Don't trust her," E.J. said. "She tells Robert everything."

"I already figured that out," Alison admitted. Office politics were not something she didn't experience at her crazy job. More and more, however, being on the sidelines seemed the only upside of her current situation. And that was a poor statement about the mess she was in.

She didn't see Jared all day, since he was in court. E.J.'s conversation left Alison feeling vulnerable and lost. She went straight home and called her mother, something she hadn't done for quite a while. When Alison wasn't on the road, she lived at home.

"I miss you," she said, after catching up on family news.

"Alison, honey, you've never said that before." Her mother's voice had a funny catch to it. "Don't tell me this gypsy life is getting to you finally. I hope, I hope."

"Yeah. A little. Maybe. I don't know."

"That's certainly clear enough."

Someone knocked on her door. "Wait a minute, Mom."

She set the phone down and peered through the door's peephole. Jared stood on the other side. Smiling, she swung the door open.

He swept her up and kissed her soundly. "Thank you. I was afraid the citizen patrol would arrest me again for returning to the scene of my crime. Why didn't you wait for me at the office? No matter. I've tracked you down." He kissed her again, then roared, "Woman! I want dessert. *Now!*"

"My mother's on the phone."

Jared dropped her like a hot potato. "Nothing kills the mood better than dear old mom."

Alison giggled and returned to her call. "I'm back."

"Tell whoever he is that I'm not *old*."

Alison turned to Jared. "Mom says she's not old."

His face flushed beet red, a charming side to a so-phisticated attorney. "Tell Mom I think she's young and beautiful, and at least I didn't put her in the grave like you did."

"Thanks," Alison muttered.

"There's a story here," her mother said over the miles from Syracuse. "And I can't wait to hear it."

What the heck was this with her personal life? Alison felt like the latest hot gossip in the *National Enquirer*. "I've got to go, Mom."

"You call me back the moment he leaves, missy. Whoever he is, he's got you missing things you've never yearned for before. I like him already."

"Goodbye, Mom," Alison said firmly, then hung up the receiver.

"Wow," Jared said. "You've actually got a mom."

"No. I fell out of a tree at birth." Alison made a face at him. "I told you about my mother."

"One of the few things you have told me, after telling me she had passed on." He waved a hand when she protested. "So what did she say?"

"She likes you. Does that make you happy?"

"Ecstatic, especially after that 'old' remark." He shed his suit jacket and came over to her. Pulling her into his embrace, he kissed her just under her ear. "So when do I meet Mom? How about this weekend? We can fly out to Chicago Friday night and come back Sunday. I'll even be a good boy and stay at a hotel nearby. How's that for chaste?"

"You don't know the meaning of the word, thank goodness. But my mother doesn't live in Chicago."

His face turned to stone, just as she realized the implications of what she'd said.

"You told me you were from Chicago," he said, letting go of her.

"That was the last place I *lived*," she replied. "I never said my family was from there."

"I think you did, but I suppose this is something else I can't ask about."

She said nothing for a long moment, her silence answering his comment. She hated all this, yet her hands were tied with her job requirements. It occurred to her that her little fantasy world could not go on. "Robert complained to E.J. about your kissing my hand. He's suspicious—"

"I don't give a damn what he is," Jared snapped.

"Well, you better," she snapped back, her own frustrations flaring.

"You assure me that you have no problems, yet you carry a gun and tell me you can't tell me anything about your life." He cut the air with one hand. "What the hell am I supposed to think?"

Just what he did, she thought. She would think the same if she were him. She had indulged in a dream by getting involved with him. She had allowed this situation to get out of control. He would hate her if he ever found out the truth. She never wanted him to hate her. The tools to rectify things before he was more hurt had been put in her hands. "I can't help what you are supposed to think, but I can help you with Robert and with your work. I don't want there to be any questions about you, or me, with him—"

"I told you I don't give a damn about Robert!" Jared retorted, his voice raised. He glared at her, his anger coming at her like waves. She could almost see them.

"You *do* give a damn about that partnership," she said. "And so do I. I think it's time for me to leave Davis, Hansen and Davis—"

"No!" He reached out and grabbed her to him. The shock of his hard, lean body sent shudders through Alison. He added, "Don't leave me, do you understand? Leaving solves nothing."

His mouth captured hers in a searing kiss that scorched her heart. She responded instinctively, wanting only to savor the taste of him before she let him go.

Finally he eased his mouth from hers. "Tell me you can leave what we have."

If he had asked anything else, she might have been able to deny the truth. But she was tired of lying to him...and to herself. "No."

His lips traced a path from the ultrasensitive skin just under her ear down her neck to the base of her throat. His kisses were in turn gentle and fierce, as if he would brand her. His lemony aftershave filled her senses, imprinting the scent of him on her brain as it always did. She could barely think, let alone speak.

"I love you," he said, raising his head. "I've loved you from the moment I saw you. I've never pushed you to say you love me back, but, dammit, tell me it means something to you!"

She wanted to, especially with what his hands were doing to her body. But his welfare came before her selfishness. "Jared, I want what's best for you."

"I decide what's best for me, and you are best for me."

"I make you unhappy," she whispered, clinging to him. "I can't tell you things, because you'll hate me. I don't want you to hate me."

"No. Never."

"Yes, you will. You will." She pressed her face against his neck. "I don't want you to hate me. I love you. I shouldn't, but I do."

She had finally said the words she'd kept hidden inside her for so long—and she felt like a louse even as they left her lips.

"Say it again," he demanded, lifting her face up so he could see it.

She looked right into his eyes, and couldn't *not* say it again. "I love you."

He kissed her so desperately she thought she would break from it. She did break. Somewhere inside her, the last shred of integrity was stripped away, and she lost control.

"Say it again. And again. And again."

She did.

"I can't wait." He backed her against the wall, flipping up her pleated skirt. He fumbled with her panty hose, finally shredding them to get the barrier off her body. Alison, wanting to unite as much as he did, yanked his shirt open, exposing his chest. She tugged at the buttons of her blouse and undid the front clasp of her bra. She rubbed her naked breasts against his body, his lightly matted chest hairs tickling her skin. His breath rasped loudly in and out of his lungs. She couldn't even find air in her own. When she wrapped her legs around his naked hips and sank onto him at last, she didn't need to breathe any longer. She only need to be part of him.

Their lovemaking was gentle and fierce like his kisses...and earthy and angelic...and filled with love. Alison cried out her love again and again when the pleasure he created tipped over the edge into sweet oblivion.

She loved him. She was doomed.

THAT SHE LOVED HIM didn't solve anything. It only made it worse.

Jared listened to the court proceedings with only half an ear as he thought about Alison. It had been a week since she'd confessed her love for him. So far, everything was the same...and yet it wasn't at all. Only when he made love with her did he feel truly connected. She responded so fervently, so intimately, that he had no doubts about her then. Outside forces kept her emotionally distant from him at all the other times. That must be it. Raymond's advice looked more and more logical. Jared *had* to know what she hid so he could help her. Nothing was bad enough to scare him away.

In the meantime, he had to keep her near him. That meant her staying at Davis, Hansen and Davis. Once she left the firm, the barn door would be open and she would truly be gone. Right this minute she could be telling E.J. to get a replacement for the microfiche room. Robert would do what Robert would do, regardless of Alison's leaving or not. Her noble action would mean nothing. Robert would simply find another excuse for awarding the partnership elsewhere if that's what he wanted.

Jared vowed to quit if Robert did award the partnership to one of the others. He was disgusted with Robert's nonsense, and this business with Alison would be the last straw.

"Mr. Holiday. Are you planning to give your opening statement sometime today?"

Judge Butkowski glared at him, the old man's eyebrows like albino twin arches on his lined face.

Jared flushed a little. He cleared his throat and rose to his feet. "Yes, your honor. This isn't a typical divorce..."

He smiled at his client as he began her cause. She had

been an exotic dancer before marrying an older, mainline maven, a powerful Philadelphian with a bank account to match his pedigree. At issue was a prenuptial agreement of ironclad proportions. Jared was positive he could break it. Having had several affairs, the husband had clearly not kept his wedding vows, for one thing. He'd promised to do so in the prenup.

Jared knew his own client had had a one-night stand with an old boyfriend after the marriage deteriorated. But his opposing counsel didn't know that.

After he finished his statements, the judge nodded *without* pursing his lips. Jared knew he'd made points, despite his late start. The husband's attorney knew it, too. Judge Butkowski was notorious for pursing his lips when he wasn't buying the argument. Like poker, if one could read the face, one had the game.

Opposing counsel stood and began his opening statement. After the man's first few sentences, Jared stopped patting himself on the back. He stopped feeling the least confident when the attorney announced they would prove the wife had not only married just for money, but had continued a long-established pattern of unfaithfulness with a former lover, thereby breaking the prenuptial agreement.

"What the hell is this?" Jared's client whispered in his ear.

"I don't know," he muttered, keeping his facial expression to a slight smirk, as if this news were nonsense. Out of the side of his mouth, he said, "Could your ex-boyfriend have said anything in revenge against you?"

"No. I *know* he didn't. He's married and doesn't want to hurt his wife. The only other person who knows is you."

His client sounded positive. Jared wondered if she should be.

"Then he's just talking, trying to shake us." And doing a damn good job of it. If his client jumped around in her chair any more, opposing counsel would know he had hit a mark and would start digging. "Calm down. Don't let them know they've got something solid."

The wife settled back, and the rest of the morning in court went well enough, for the opening. But Jared had a bad feeling about the attorney's promise.

He had a worse feeling when he got back to the office and Robert called him on the carpet. Jared's client had no sooner left court than she lodged a complaint about breach of confidentiality with Robert.

"I didn't breach a damn thing," Jared replied, disgusted with the entire episode. "The ex-boyfriend probably told the husband, out of revenge. It happens."

"You better hope that's what happened," Robert said. "If it comes from your office, it's malpractice, and I'm not having it!"

"I guarantee my office's integrity."

"It's on your head if you can't."

When Jared finally did reach his office, he slammed the door shut in frustration. He called the husband's attorney to get some answers. There was such a thing as discovery and reporting it to the other side, even in divorce cases.

"Jim, what's all this crap about 'longtime pattern of unfaithfulness?'" Jared asked bluntly. "You know you can't prove it."

"I think I can. I just discovered she's got an ex-boyfriend who may not be so ex."

"You're supposed to declare that *before* bringing it up in court. You breach discovery, and I'll nail you."

"I just got a lead on it, and I'm looking into it. Don't worry, I'm not breaching anything—and you know it."

Jared hung up the phone and thought for a while. He got out his client's files and was surprised to see Alison had been the one to type up the case notes on her first day. If the client was right that the ex-boyfriend wouldn't talk about the one-night stand, then besides himself, only Alison knew about it, and the breach would have to have come from either of them.

Jared could vouch for himself.

She wouldn't have, he thought, after the first disturbing notion went through his head. He disliked having the finger even pointed her way. Yet if his client was right about who knew and who would never tell…

Raymond's words haunted him. *Find out.*

Jared met up with Alison after work, at her place. The sparse, cheap furnishings burned into his brain. What was she hiding? Why would she think he'd hate her if he found out?

Was it this? Had she been bribed to leak information? Had she been a planted spy in the first place? It could explain a lot of her actions and protests.

Jared hated himself for even thinking such a thing about her. How could he love her and think she was that?

"What's wrong?" Alison asked, when she set dinner in front of him. She was having just the vegetables from the chicken stir-fry she'd made. "You're very quiet tonight."

He thought about confronting her outright, but knew he'd get nowhere. That method hadn't worked yet, anyway. "Just thinking, I guess."

"Rough day in court?"

The question sounded so domestic and innocent. Any

other time he'd love the question. Today, however, it seemed more probing, more knowledgeable of the reply, more personal.

"Yes, as a matter of fact, I did," he answered, picking at the chicken pieces on his plate. "It looks like I've had a confidentiality breach with one of my clients."

Her eyes widened. "Oh, no! What happened? Can you talk about it? I understand if you can't."

"Interestingly, with you I can. You typed up some notes about it on your first day with us." He explained what had happened, watching her face for any betrayal of knowledge.

She showed none. Either she was innocent or she had one of the finest poker faces he'd ever seen.

"The ex-boyfriend must have told," Alison said when he was done relating the day's events.

"Why do you say that?"

"Well, what else could it be? The wife wouldn't have told the husband about her one mistake. You certainly didn't. The ex-boyfriend is the only logical choice."

"I suppose."

"You sound dubious."

He felt dubious as hell. "My client guarantees he was silent. As you say, she wouldn't tell, and she wouldn't guarantee the guy if she weren't sure. I *know* I was silent. It's my job to be. This could cost us the case." He cleared his throat. "Could you have *accidentally* said anything? Maybe you didn't realize it was confidential. I know some of that stuff was a real eye-opener, especially on your first day—"

"Jared, I have no one to talk to, let alone about work," she said. "It definitely wasn't me. I know how to mind my own business. I could give lessons on the subject, believe me."

She gazed at him steadily, but her look spoke volumes about her annoyance at even being questioned—and it spoke about her disappointment that he doubted her integrity. Jared dropped the subject with an "OK."

Only his brain couldn't quite drop the other questions about her, ones that never were answered and never went away.

That night he didn't ask anything further of her than her physical presence. Dredging up the questions of her soon leaving him would bring one answer he didn't want. He didn't even ask her to repeat that she loved him when they made love. He wanted her to say it without his prompting for once. She didn't.

It hurt.

At three in the morning, while she slept against his side, Jared stared at the darkened ceiling, just as he had for long, miserable hours. His life had been turned upside down since Alison arrived on his office doorstep Labor Day. He was no closer, despite an intimate relationship with her, than he had been back then, months ago.

Today was Halloween, and he needed answers. He knew Raymond was right. It was time to unmask Alison. She might hate him, but he had to take the risk. The doubts had piled up too high to ignore any longer.

Slowly, gently, carefully, he eased away from her.

She didn't wake when he crawled out of bed and onto the floor. Maybe Alison was a Japanese spy in disguise, he thought facetiously, his bones creaking a little from the futonlike arrangement she had for a bed.

He found his trousers and crept out of the room, pulling the bedroom door shut behind him. He put on the trousers out in the hallway, then padded into Alison's kitchen. He flipped on the small, florescence light over

the sink, giving the room a dull, eerily white glow
among its dark shadows.

He had intended to call the firm's detective agency
and leave a message with the answering service for a
breakfast meeting with the agency's head man. Now that
Jared had made up his mind, he wanted to immediately
begin the process of tracking down the real Alison.

Alison's large purse caught his eye first. That same
purse had already told him much when he'd found her
gun in it. Maybe it could tell him a whole lot more about
her.

If he looked.

He would be invading her privacy, a little voice ar-
gued. He would be wrong to snoop. On the other hand,
maybe he'd find answers that would ease his turmoil.
Maybe he'd at least get some information that would
help do so. He definitely wanted his turmoil eased.

If he was willing to have the detective find out about
her, he ought to at least be willing to soil his hands and
dig a little himself.

He opened the purse and set the gun on the kitchen
counter. The last thing he needed was the damn thing
going off while he rooted around in her bag. He took
out her wallet and undid the clasp.

What he found inside stunned him.

Buried among several credit cards—gold credit
cards—was an FBI identification card. Jared lifted it up
to the light, reading it carefully while hoping what he'd
read at first glance had been a crazy mistake.

Alison's name was prominently displayed on the card.
So was her picture. She had pulled her abundant hair
into a bun at the nape, he guessed, for it looked tightly
drawn to her scalp. But the photo was certainly Alison,
along with her height, weight and general description.

The government seal looked as genuine as any he had seen before, and he had seen several.

Alison was an FBI agent?

The room tilted wildly as Jared's head spun from the revelation he held in his hand. His stomach dropped sickeningly and his knees turned to water. After an eternity of emotions, the room finally righted itself.

Alison was an FBI agent.

Jared stormed into the bedroom, snapping on the overhead light. Brightness flooded the room. He kicked the foot of the mattress, shoved the card in Alison's sleepy face and borrowed a line from his angry, exotic-dancer client.

"What the hell is this?"

Chapter Twelve

Alison blinked, the sudden blinding light, earthquake jolt to the bed and Jared's voice piercing through her sleep.

She realized it was the middle of the night. She realized he held something in his hand. She realized what it was.

Her bureau ID card.

Alison shrieked, horrified at what he must have done. "Where did you get that?"

"Your bag. It was among the gold credit cards, Ms. Moneybags. Or are they fake, too?"

"No." She sat up, pulling the covers over her nakedness. Her stomach churned. "Dammit, you had no right to go in my purse. *No* right!"

He glared at her. "What the hell are you? Is this another lie or are you really an FBI agent?"

She tried to calm herself, to think straight. The damage was done; she'd been "outed." But how to explain herself? She didn't know how, without Jared hating her. She also had to keep the other damage at a minimum.

"Yes, I'm an agent," she said, knowing she at least owed him the truth. She was so tired of lying to him. She was so tired of it all.

He stared at her, his jaw dropping.

"Don't look so surprised," she said, hating herself for turning on him as she was now. "You have the card in your hand."

"Somehow I didn't think it was real. You're too ditzy to be an FBI agent."

"We're not all Scullys from *X-Files,* you know."

"You're not a decorator," he said.

"I'm color-blind."

"Color-blind! Then how can you be an agent?"

She rubbed her fingers on the bedspread for a moment. "I cheated on the eye test."

"Cheated?"

She hated herself for this, too, her one desperate deception to get into the bureau in the first place. "During my initial physical, I recognized the general pattern test from high school. Eye doctors rarely change them, you know, so I took a chance and I guessed right. I wasn't going into criminal investigative work, anyway, where I might have harmed something with my color blindness." She smiled wryly. "If I really did redecorate your house without a picture and specific manufacturers, it would have been a disaster. That's why I stalled so much."

"You're unreal," he said, the disgust easy to read on his face.

She gazed at him, knowing she finally faced the moment she had tried so hard to avoid. But she wouldn't run from it any longer. "Jared, there's a lot of things going on that you won't understand but I need to tell you."

"Just tell me if you're investigating the firm. Are you investigating me?" He laughed bitterly. "You know more than most."

"No. Well, yes, in a way, but not really." She knew

she sounded confusing. Pushing her hair back from her face, she said, "Can I get up and make some coffee for you and some tea for me? I'm going to need a clear head for this."

"No. I'm not letting you anywhere near that gun of yours."

"Jared, I would never shoot you!" she exclaimed, outraged. "I love you."

He said nothing for a long moment. "Just tell me what's going on here."

She sighed. "I work for the bureau in a special operations branch of the witness-protection program. The government supports federal witnesses financially for only so long in their new life. We haven't done the best job in the past of putting people into communities where they match up well emotionally and culturally, and where they can eventually support themselves. Covers have been blown because of it. The bureau began a team that would scope out an area or region, live the life of the residents, to get the feel of the people and the economics. I'm a member of that team."

He scowled. "You're telling me you live like everyone else, then report whether it's good enough to the government? I don't believe it."

"It's true. People have no clue about their neighbors and their co-workers," Alison said. "That's why the witnesses can be given a new life with a clean slate. But someone has to make sure they'll do well in a placement when the government foundations are gone. Reading local newspapers just hasn't cut it. Frankly, local FBI offices have had problems in the past with corruption. The program I'm in is disassociated from any problems like that. Can you honestly say you know who your neighbors are?"

"I thought I knew who you were. I don't."

"You know me," she said, reaching out to touch his arm. "Jared, you know who I am."

He flinched away from her. "I thought you were in trouble. I feel stupid now."

"You were very sweet—"

"Very stupid. I was a big, dumb, hulking, would-be hero." He grimaced. "All my life I thought women needed help. Women don't. Raymond's right. Women are manipulators. You made me a fool, Alison."

"Jared, no, you're not."

"The hell I'm not! I was just a little fun fling for you while you're in town."

"Jared, no," she began, her body shaking with fear at what was coming.

"You must have laughed like hell over doing my office. Color-blind! Damn good thing you used a picture, otherwise that would have been a disaster, too."

"I tried to warn you."

"So you did." He stared at her, the hurt in his expression too painful for Alison to bear. "This apartment is a lie, isn't it? That's why it has no furniture. What else is a lie, Alison? No money—that's one we've already established. You've got to be paid very well to have gold cards."

"Some are the bureau's."

"Was Mom a lie that day on the telephone?"

"No. That was her. She lives in Syracuse." Pleading, Alison said, "Jared, I didn't want to lie about anything but I had to hide my real life, what I do. You kept asking questions and picking up on background things and running with them—"

"Oh, so now it's my fault you lied to me. I bet your birthday's a lie, too."

"It's in July," she admitted in a low voice.

"And that one's my fault, too. And the brother? And your dead father? What are they? Since they're my fault, I ought to know whether I created a lie or not."

"It's not your fault, OK? It's mine. And I do have a brother in Syracuse, and my father did pass away." She wanted to defend herself more, but felt like an incredible hypocrite. "I'm adopted—"

"Adopted!" He laughed hysterically.

"Yes, adopted." Maybe if he knew about her past, he'd understand her better. "My biological father was a witness in the sixties for some of the first mob trials. He was killed before he could testify and before I was born. My birth mother gave me up for adoption. She died shortly afterward. I do what I do, Jared, because I want to see others be safe, the way my parents weren't."

He shook his head. "So why pick on Davis, Hansen and Davis? We don't handle underworld-criminal defenses."

"I didn't 'pick' on your firm. I was randomly assigned there as a temp. *You* called the temp service, remember? I temp to get the feel of an area, to see what types of jobs are available, so we can match people up better in the program." She added, "Jared, what I do can't get out to anybody. The success of the program depends on its covert operation. I wanted to tell you so many times, but I couldn't. I wasn't allowed to. I shouldn't even be telling you this now."

"What was I?" he asked. "The test lay of Philadelphia?"

"That's enough!" Alison snapped. "I shouldn't have become personally involved with you. I know that."

"You were always going to leave, weren't you? I

could have told you I loved you until I was blue in the face and it wouldn't have mattered.''

"It does matter. A lot.''

Jared cursed. He flung the bureau card at her and picked up the rest of his clothes from her floor. "You disgust me, Alison....''

His rejection hurt more than she'd thought anything ever would. "Jared, please. I never meant to hurt you.''

He paused. "I bet not. You just planned to go without a word. Don't worry, I won't tell anyone about you. No one would believe it, and I'd look like a complete idiot again. I'm through with that crap.''

He left her with those hideous words and slammed out of her apartment.

Alison listened to the silence for a long moment, then rolled over and buried her face in her pillow. Jared's scent lingered on the case.

She cried.

JARED ENTERED his office the next day, feeling as though he'd had a nightmare of epic proportions.

He'd awakened in his own bed alone this morning after a fitful night, but he wasn't reassured he'd originally started out there. Unfortunately, he knew damn well he hadn't dreamed the whole scene with Alison.

He stared at his little statue of Justice, the woman of his ideals. She was real in what she stood for. Oh, others might abuse the attributes she set forth, but that didn't alter her or her meaning.

What a jerk he had been—and he must have looked like an even bigger jerk, running around trying to protect her from evil forces in the universe.

Jared wiped his face with his hands, pulling down on

the skin while wishing he could erase the humiliation he felt with the gesture.

He didn't want to believe Alison's latest story, but the ID card, the credit cards, the gun, the silence, even her job here all clicked together in a far better fit—a near-perfect fit—compared to anything he'd dreamed up about her.

But she should have told him the truth from the beginning. She should have trusted him.

That hurt worst of all.

His phone rang. Robert was on the line, to further bedevil him, no doubt.

"Your client has lodged a formal complaint with the ABA and the ATA."

Jared cursed. The American Bar Association and the Association of Trial Attorneys meant big trouble. "Dammit, I *never* leaked anything to her husband's attorney. Why would I destroy my own case?"

"That does seem illogical." Robert sounded almost sympathetic. Almost. His next comment killed any notion of Robert having a heart. "I'm suspending you indefinitely from the firm, however."

"What?" Jared exclaimed, shocked.

"I want no scandal to touch this firm. I've protected it for far too long to have it sabotaged by your carelessness now."

"Did you ever hear of standing by your employees, Robert?" Jared asked.

"Not in a situation like this."

"There is no situation, dammit! I have cases to be tried, including one this afternoon."

"I'm asking for continuances in all your cases until I can get them transferred to other staff attorneys. You're off them all until further notice."

"Thank you for judging me by the Napoleonic Code, Robert." Jared banged the receiver down on the telephone.

He wondered what else could go wrong with his life.

"Not much," he muttered.

Deciding on a course of action, he made copies of some of his computer files, ones he felt it imperative to have. Then he realized he could take the tape-drive backup copy of the entire disk drive, instead. After the missing billings, he'd learned how to operate it and was a pro now. The tape backup had a copy of *everything* on the computer since yesterday. He'd be better off with all his files. He put the tape in his briefcase. He also added his Rolodex and the Justice statue.

He left his office and headed for the miles-of-files room. He hadn't seen Alison this morning and hadn't expected to. She would be long gone, now that her "cover" was blown. She'd been threatening to leave, and he had no doubt last night provided the impetus. At least he could get some of his back files, without her presence. To hell with company policy regarding taking files upon dismissal, he thought. He was still technically employed by Davis, Hansen and Davis. Robert could bust a gut over that all he wanted.

Alison was in the file room.

Jared stopped dead and stared at her as she sat hunched over the microfilm machine. He couldn't believe she was still with the firm.

She wore a severe black suit and had braided her hair back from her face. The suit hugged her curves in earthy fashion and the braid made her face sensual—hardly crisp, business looks.

She gazed at him. His heart beat faster, almost painfully in his chest. Dark circles ringed her eyes, as if she was hurting. The thought didn't give him the satisfaction he would have expected, after being betrayed. Reminded that her looks had been deceiving all along, he forced himself to calm down.

"I thought you would be gone," he said, recognizing that they were alone in the file room.

"I was hired to do a job here, and I won't just vanish from it. That wouldn't be fair," she said. Her voice lowered. "Jared, I'm sorry—"

"Don't," he interrupted. "I don't need to hear it. What you did was unforgivable. You lied about everything."

"I lied only when I had to."

"It doesn't matter," he said. "I was nothing but temporary sex for you."

"That's not true!"

He snorted. "Tell me that when you're here ten years. I might believe you then. *Might*. I will throw you a bone and tell you I do believe you didn't leak that confidential information to the husband. With your background and with your real purpose here, that's as ludicrous as your only lying when you had to."

She sat tall, her gaze sharpening. "I'd say thank you but you're having too much fun in your martyrdom."

"Yeah, I'm right up there with St. Andrew, especially since I've been suspended from the firm today, too. It only adds to the fun. But don't worry. That wasn't you, either. A miracle."

He walked down the aisles and began pulling files he knew he might need in the future. He concentrated on the billing files. His salary and bonuses were based on them.

Alison caught up to him. "Jared, wait! You were suspended? What for?"

"What the hell do you care?"

"With your attitude, I'm wondering the same thing. But I do care. What happened?"

He didn't want to tell her. He didn't want to care what she thought. But he couldn't stop himself. "My client lodged a formal complaint with the ABA and the ATA. Robert decided to hang me out to dry."

"But that's totally unfair," Alison said, her outrage evident in her expression. "You would never give over the information. And I didn't, so it didn't come from your office."

"No kidding." He pulled a couple more files from the shelf and set them in his briefcase, then snapped the locks closed.

"What are you doing?" she asked.

"Taking files I need. Why? Are you going to pull your gun and shoot me for stealing?"

"Not me. I only work here." She continued, "It had to have been the boyfriend...or maybe the wife inadvertently said what she shouldn't have. Maybe that's why she lodged a formal complaint. Lots of people would rather blame anybody else than look to themselves as the problem. I hope you're fighting back."

He shrugged.

Her jaw dropped in clear astonishment. "Jared! You've got to fight this!"

"Robert's done the unforgivable as far as I'm concerned." He gazed at her, then added, "Nothing in my life is reliable. Especially you."

Alison looked as stricken as she had last night when he'd shoved her FBI card under his nose. OK, so she might feel bad for lying to him, he thought. But that couldn't change what she had done. How could he trust anything from her again?

He couldn't.

Jared walked out of the file room, walked out of Davis, Hansen and Davis and walked away from Alison Palmer.

No doubt about it, he decided. This was the worst day of his life.

ALISON SNIFFED BACK fresh tears.

She had to stop crying, she thought. Crying couldn't make up for what she had done to Jared. Besides, the microfiche material turned to a blur when she cried.

She had made this mess; she deserved his contempt. She hadn't asked to leave the job here, hoping to see Jared, hoping to explain to him further, hoping for forgiveness…hoping against hope. At least he hadn't said he hated her. But he must.

Worse, he was in deep trouble with his job.

Her heart went out to him. She wanted so much to help him somehow. She wanted to make up for lying to him all this time. The ex-boyfriend had to have told, she thought. That was the most logical explanation.

The incident of the earlier missing billing files popped into her head. Poor Jared. He had had a lot of bad luck lately.

But how they'd gone missing was so strange, she admitted. Not only the hard copy but the computer files as well. Now he had another sinister happening on top of it, and all when he was vying for a firm partnership....

That was a lot of coincidence.

Her brain, trained to be suspicious, took up the thread that the two happenings weren't coincidence. She wondered what it would mean if the client was right about the boyfriend keeping silent, as well as the woman's conviction of her own closed mouth. If neither of them had leaked the short affair, nor had Jared or Alison herself, then who could have? Who would have the incentive to do so?

"Eliminate all that you can and whatever remains, no matter how improbable, is the answer," she said out loud, paraphrasing her all-time-favorite detective, Sherlock Holmes.

The improbable here was someone else in the office, who would have access to the case notes.

But why would anyone from the firm trash Jared's files or give them over to the opposition? The latter could cost the entire firm big money in a malpractice suit. Something would have to outweigh that.

E.J. came into the file room. "I don't believe this place! Jared got suspended!"

"I know," Alison said. "He told me."

E.J.'s eyebrows shot up. "He told you? Nobody's seen him this morning. I heard about it from Robert, who's being too damn smug about suspending him, although the weasel wouldn't say why. Do you know?"

Alison nodded, but hesitated telling the story to E.J.

"Give over, girl."

She was still reluctant but did tell, hoping E.J. might be able to push Jared's cause with people in the office.

"That's ridiculous!" E.J. said. "Jared has *never* had anything happen like this before. We should be backing him, not suspending him. Between his missing quarterly billing and the leak, his work biorhythms must be in the toilet...or someone's out to get him—"

"Could someone be?" Alison asked, jumping on the notion so similar to her own.

E.J. gaped at her.

Alison waved her hand. "It's a wild notion I had. Probably the client or the client's friends must have said something that put the husband's attorney on the track. We know Jared didn't, and I was temping for him and typed up that file, so I *know* it wasn't me." She swallowed a sudden lump of tears. "E.J., I love him—"

"Hot damn!" E.J. said, her face lighting up. "I knew it!"

"Well, forget it. He hates me now. He has reason to, and don't ask why because I will not tell you that. It's between him and me. But how can I help him? I would gladly go away nice and quiet like a little mouse if I knew he was OK."

"There's a story in this," E.J. said. "And I *will* get it out of you."

"Not in my lifetime. Can Jared be helped? What can I do for him?"

"I don't know." E.J. shook her head. "This kills his partnership chances. In fact, he's out on his ear from that already. After the suspension is over, he'll never be considered again at Davis, Hansen and Davis. That's too big a black mark to overcome...."

Things clicked into place as E.J. talked. Alison suddenly had a very fine reason to explain the improbable. Someone wanted Jared out of the running for the partnership. Maybe out of consideration forever. Maybe even out of the firm.

But who? Who hated Jared so much to do this to him? Robert came to mind. So did another type of who. The type who wanted or needed the partnership so bad, he or she would go to such lengths to get it.

Granted, Alison was not on the investigative side of the bureau, but she'd been trained in those procedures. She could think of no better time to put her training to good use. Maybe, if she helped vindicate Jared, she could make up for what she'd done to him.

After E.J. left, Alison got to work.

ON THE THIRD DAY of his suspension, Jared paced his living room like a caged tiger.

Half of him still burned over being suspended. The other half burned over Alison's betrayal.

He avoided looking at the baby grand, its presence reminding him too sharply of the night Alison had played. And slept in his bed.

Why had she stayed on at the firm?

Finishing a job seemed so illogical, he thought. Certainly she didn't have to remain with Davis, Hansen and Davis to do her FBI work.

He didn't understand her. He certainly couldn't trust her again. Yet he wondered what he would have done if he had been in her position. If only she had been on some noble investigation and couldn't tell him, then he might have been able to accept her deceptions. But on a routine job of scoping out a region? How could anyone accept that deception? He was making himself crazy even thinking about her.

His doorbell rang, the first interruption to his enforced retreat.

Alison stood on the other side of the door when he opened it. He gaped at her, shocked to find her here.

"Can I come in for a minute?" she asked. "I have something I think you ought to see."

He opened his door wider, although his emotions warred about whether it was a wise idea to be in her presence.

The brisk November air had brought out the color in her cheeks. Her eyes seemed to sparkle more than usual, and her strawberry blond hair tumbled past her shoulders with shining health. He wanted to kiss the chill from her lips. He wanted to do more.

She wore a purple coat that looked more like a cape the way it swung from her slender body. Her heather plaid skirt peeked out from underneath. One more time when she hardly looked like what she was, he thought. And yet one more time did she look like the Alison he'd loved from the day they had met.

She pulled off mittens and flexed her fingers. "I think we're going to have a cold winter." She made a face. "I'm sure you don't want small talk from me. I came because I have something you need to see."

She reached in her big tote bag and pulled out some papers. She handed them over.

Their fingers touched. Jared glanced up to her face. Alison's blue eyes were wide with emotion. He felt as jolted as she looked.

He managed to take the papers without showing his vulnerability. "What is this?"

"A printout of the activities of your computer modem."

He looked at it. Numbers and words could be blurred together for all he understood them. "What does it mean?"

"It tells what connections have been made to and from your modem and what time they occurred. You don't have very many, but the ones you have are interesting."

He frowned. "Where did you get this?"

She grinned. "Let's just say I had to work late. I checked up on a few ideas I had. I accessed your computer through your modem and printed that out. Jared, it was dead easy. Do you have *any* clue how to secure your computer?"

"No."

"It shows. It's on all the time, for one thing, and you have no secured files, besides."

"I told you before that I'm a computer dummy. I know I have a modem and a separate phone line for it, partly to be on the Internet, although I've barely used that. The computer company that has our maintenance contract uses the modem to work on our computers from their repair center. Are you saying they got my stuff through my modem?"

"Not them." She pointed to the paper. "Someone inside Davis, Hansen and Davis got to your files. See these numbers? That's from a telephone line assigned to the firm, not an outside line. Do you know it?"

"Not offhand. How did you find this out?"

She grinned. "I have connections with the phone company. I come in handy occasionally."

"But what does this mean?" he asked, feeling incredibly dumb. "What's the point of my modem and accessing files?"

He knew he sounded sarcastic, but he couldn't help it.

"Someone made transfers *twice,* using your modem. They took the quarterly billing." She pointed. "See? They were on for over a half hour, probably looking for the files and then transferring them. It's showing a large data transfer. That's where your entire billing directory went." She paused in her musing and pointed again. "Here's where they went after your client's case-file notes. It's very close to the date of the court date. They probably copied that file, leaving the original in place so everything looked OK. I'm also betting they had more in mind, but Robert suspended you."

Jared stared at the paper. Slowly, the information became clear to him. He still couldn't believe what she was suggesting.

"But why would someone want to go after my files? I don't have anything of importance—"

"Yes, you do. You have things your opposing counsels would want, for one thing. Maybe someone bribed someone in the firm to get your case notes, although I doubt that's what is behind that. But more important, aren't you a candidate for a partnership with the firm? Davis, Hansen and Davis is a very successful law firm. I bet the partners make millions. Am I wrong?"

"No. That's where the money is with any firm."

"There you go. Someone doesn't want you to be a partner."

"I can't believe either Mark, Bill or Margaret would sabotage me to better their own candidacies. They have always been ethical."

"The culprit's here." She tapped the paper at the modem number. "The person who has that line. Drew Goldwyn, the accounts-receivable manager for the firm."

"That's impossible!" Jared said, floored by her suggestion. "Why would he have it in for me? He's not up for the partnership. He's Robert's toady, but that has nothing to do with me."

"Why he did it, I can't answer. I can only give you the facts. But isn't it convenient that he never 'received' your hard copy of the billing? I think you need to take this to Robert now, so you can vindicate yourself."

"But I don't have proof he actually did this."

"You have proof his computer accessed yours. Show this to Robert and get him to have Drew's computer checked. I bet we might find the files there. It's worth a shot. If nothing else, he'll have a very hard time explaining why your computer was accessed by his.''

Dubious himself about what had happened, Jared stared at the papers a moment longer, then looked up into her gaze. ''Why did you do this?''

She glanced away, tightening her jaw as she did. Finally she answered, ''I owed you for what happened. I wouldn't feel right if I didn't help you.''

Paybacks were a bitch, he thought, wishing she still ''owed'' him. Her no longer owing him meant closure to their relationship. Suddenly, he hated closure.

''You better go see Robert right now,'' she said.

''You better come with me,'' he replied. ''I think I'm going to need you to explain to Robert.''

He put his hand on her back to usher her out...and nearly pulled her into his embrace. How could he still want her after all that had happened? He was like an automaton when it came to Alison.

He drove them both to the firm, not saying much along the way. He was too busy mulling over what she'd found and why she had searched for it.

As he and Alison strode toward Robert's office, Jared decided not to wait to be announced. He had a premonition that if he did, Robert would let him kick his heels for an hour before allowing him in. Instead Jared asked the secretary if Robert was in and alone, then walked past her and opened the door. The secretary trailed behind Alison, squawking in protest.

Robert half rose from his chair. ''What is this?''

Jared shook the paper Alison had given him under Robert's nose. ''This is my backing, Robert, support of my credibility that the firm chose *not* to give to me. You better listen before I go to the bar association and lodge my own formal complaint against the firm.''

Robert frowned and waved his secretary away. He glanced at Alison. "You can go, too."

"Oh, no." Jared put his arm around her. "Alison stays. She discovered what happened to my billing and where the leak is. I'll let her explain it to you."

Alison gave Jared a sharp glance, then took the modem information from him. She spread it out on Robert's desk and explained what it was and what it meant. She added a few more details, especially about his missing billing directory and her suspicions. She was cool, logical and concise. Jared smiled, proud as hell of her—and more than grateful. One thing she didn't say was whose modem number it was. He wondered at that and nearly accused the accounts-receivable manager himself, but sensed Alison was leading to something.

Robert, to his credit, listened patiently until she was finished, then said, "All this is very fine—if it's true— but it *proves* nothing."

At least he wasn't screaming denials.

"I believe it proves that Jared's computer was accessed by an unauthorized person two critical times, Mr. Davis. In each case, Jared was directly hurt by information taken from it."

"What would I find if I called this number?" Robert asked.

"Another computer," she said, without directly answering him. "One that I believe holds Jared's information. It may still be there, but secured, probably." She glanced at Jared. "However, I understand you use a computer company to maintain your computers. They probably have a password that would bypass the security, so they can work on the system. As the head of the firm, you should have that password. Do you?"

"Yes, but I don't know how to use it."

"Alison does," Jared said, catching her grin.

"May I?" she asked, gesturing to his chair.

Robert pursed his lips. "Why should I believe any of this? You could have set up whatever I'm going to find here, Jared, to clear yourself."

Jared bristled. "That's ridiculous. I didn't set anything up and Alison certainly wouldn't."

"Righteous outrage means nothing. And as for this woman, I am well aware of your *personal* relationship with her. She's your lover and she would do anything you say."

"I'm not his lover, and he's no Svengali, believe me," Alison said firmly. She reached in her purse and took out her wallet.

"Alison, no," Jared said, realizing what she was about to do.

She smiled and opened her wallet, handing over her identification card. "I'm an FBI agent, Mr. Davis."

Robert's jaw dropped. Jared smothered a grin, even though he didn't like her revealing herself to Robert.

Alison continued, "Although I am here at your firm, I assure you I am not on any official investigation of you, your firm, your staff or any of your clients. My interest is in another area entirely. I looked into Jared's troubles strictly as a personal favor, but I hope my revealing myself like this will reassure you of my veracity."

Damn, Jared thought in awe. She was all-business tough.

Robert read her bureau card carefully. "Why are you here if you aren't investigating anyone or anything at my firm?"

"I'm afraid I can't tell you that."

"Then I can't believe you."

"Believe her," Jared said.

Alison glanced over at him, then said to Robert, "You can verify my employment by calling the Washington bureau. Directory assistance will give you the number, if you don't want me to. Ask for Art Mallowan at Special Services. He'll verify me."

Robert did call. Jared wasn't surprised, but he could see the momentary dismay on Alison's face. After Robert spoke to her boss, he handed over the receiver to her. She gave terse, one-word answers to obviously painful questions before handing the receiver back to Robert. Jared had no doubt she had put her own job on the line for him—the job she had hidden from him, from everyone, for so long.

"All right, young lady," Robert said, after he hung up the telephone. "You are who you say you are."

Alison nodded.

"Did you know she was with the FBI?" Robert asked Jared.

"Not until recently," he replied. He glared at Alison. "Dammit, I don't want you losing your job over me."

She smiled wryly. "Which one?"

"Both."

She shrugged, then turned to Robert. "I hope you will believe me now."

Robert motioned to his chair. "All right, young lady. I'll get you that password."

Alison called up Drew Goldwyn's computer. Robert's expression didn't change when it became obvious the answering computer was his accounting manager's. Alison found where the quarterly billing directory and files were buried, along with the client-case-file notes. She also showed Robert when the files had been last opened in Drew Goldwyn's computer, each time clearly *before* the incidents took place.

Jared's anger burned. He'd taken Alison more on faith than belief over the files. But now looking at them, on Goldwyn's computer, infuriated him. He wanted to put his hands around the man's neck and squeeze. It was all he could do to stand there and look at the evidence of attempted career destruction.

"I don't know if you can alter these dates," she said, drawing his focus back. She pointed to the screen, at the dates showing the last opening of the files. "But I doubt it, unless you're a programming expert and you alter the original programming."

"How do you know all this if you are *not* an expert?" Robert asked.

"Anyone who works a lot with computers can read directory-file information. That's all this is, generated by the programs themselves. I think we're lucky he hasn't yet eliminated them from his files. I think maybe he was afraid to."

"Robert, there's a problem at Davis, Hansen and Davis and it's not me," Jared said. "I don't understand why he did this to me."

"*If* he did," Robert said. "I will have an expert examine Roger's computer for tampering. But this doesn't alter anything for you, Jared. *You* are the one responsible for your files. No one else."

Jared gritted his teeth and counted to ten. "*You* are responsible for the conduct of the members of this firm, and one of them tampered with my files and leaked damaging information to an opposing counsel. One thing you better do, Robert, is get that formal complaint against me dropped or I will lodge one against the firm. In the meantime I am calling my former client and telling her what happened here. Then I'm going to see if I can work out a settlement between her and her husband."

"Clean out your desk while you're at it," Robert said.

Jared retrieved the original paper Alison had brought to his house. "Too late. I quit. I should have known your ego would never allow you to admit you made a mistake. I expect the full severance I'm entitled to by my contract by the end of business today and reimbursement for my office refurbishing. Otherwise, you'll be hearing from *my* attorney. Alison?"

Jared stood back while she rose from the chair and preceded him from the office. It felt good to have her by his side in all this.

The first person they ran into outside was Drew Goldwyn.

Jared pinned the man up against the wall, his arm at Drew's throat. "Bastard! You stole my files and used them against me."

Roger's eyes bulged, whether from fright or lack of air was yet to be determined.

Alison tugged at Jared's arm. "Jared, I can save your butt from a lot of things, but murder, no matter how justified, isn't one of them, OK? Let him down easy."

Jared glared at her, but loosened his hold. To Drew, he said, "Why? Just tell me why."

Drew crumbled. "I'm over fifty, and you took my last chance at a partnership. The partners like you too much, but I figured Robert would pick me at the last minute if you were out of it."

Jared realized how pathetic the man was and released him. "Better ask yourself why Robert didn't get you a nomination in the first place. He'll never get you one now."

Jared took Alison's arm and walked away.

"Thanks," he said, as they left the building.

"For what?" she asked. "Robert fired you."

"I quit first. Alison, you never should have used your FBI status with Robert."

She shrugged. "It didn't much matter, when you were in so much trouble with the firm. Justice seemed more important. It still does."

"What did your boss say?" he asked.

"Well…" She sighed. "It looks like I'm behind you in the unemployment line."

"Alison!" Jared exclaimed, stunned. He'd thought she might get in some trouble, not get fired from her job because of him. "Let me call your boss and get you reinstated."

"Actually, I'm not feeling as bad about it as I thought I would," she admitted, smiling. "I think I'm even feeling good. Maybe my mom is right and I've been yearning for some things I hadn't missed before. Maybe that's why I made all those background mistakes. Maybe, unconsciously, I wanted a way out. Whatever, I certainly can't be effective any longer on the job, so it's better for all that I'm out."

"What will you do now?" he asked, the question suddenly the most imperative in his entire life.

"Well…what will you do now?" she asked in return.

He chuckled. "Good question."

He realized that he could let her walk away and never see her again. He also realized he'd be the world's biggest fool if he did.

"Robert and Drew might have done me a favor, too," he began. "I was about to do something incredibly stupid and that was let you get away. Do you think you could marry an unemployed man who may never get a job in his chosen career again? I asked you to marry me once before, when I first met you, but I'll understand if you thought I had better prospects then.''

Her eyes widened, then teared. "You really did ask me, Jared."

"If that's a 'yes,' I accept." He gazed at her, hoping her tears were good news.

"Only if you think you can marry an unemployed woman who's color-blind, has *no* career prospects and whose nose might match Pinocchio's."

Jared kissed her, keeping her tight against him. He tried in the kiss to tell her how sorry he was. And how much he loved her.

Finally, he lifted his head and grinned. "You make life exciting, especially when you decorate."

She chuckled around happy tears. "I could go back in and decorate Robert's office. That would be great revenge."

"I'm not that cruel." Jared pulled her back into his embrace and kissed her again, savoring the feel of her in his arms and her open mouth questing, tender and passionate under his.

"I love you," Alison whispered, when he eased his lips from hers for a moment.

"I love you, too," he whispered back.

He didn't need to know any more than this. He never had, not from the first moment he'd seen her.

He'd loved her at first sight and that was enough for him.

EPILOGUE

Alison was content with a small wedding.

Jared was content with a quick wedding.

He wanted her tied to him as fast as possible, he admitted, when the small service in his living room was over. Thanksgiving was only a week away, so he supposed this was fast enough. Alison had been elusive ever since their first meeting three months ago. He needed to ensure she wasn't going anywhere for the rest of her life—or his.

She wore her blue suit, one of the ones she'd bought the night of her "birthday." She'd be his blue-suit lady forever, he thought, although he grinned at the concept. Leave it to Alison to wear the unexpected for their wedding.

He kissed her with all the passion he could muster, not caring about the knot of people standing behind him. When he finally ended the kiss, applause broke out among their guests.

"Whew!" Alison said, her mouth looking deliciously bruised. "I can't wait for the honeymoon."

"Me, neither." He whispered in her ear, "Meet you upstairs in five minutes for a preview."

"Very tempting…but you explain our absence to my mother."

"Good point."

The honeymoon was taking place upstairs anyway, since neither of them were employed at the moment. He still couldn't get over how Alison had given up her job to save his—given up her commitment to the bureau, really. She had been dedicated to her job for so long. All his anger and hurt had eased at her actions on his behalf. No man could ask more of a woman. With hindsight, he could easily understand why she had hid herself from him. He'd even roared with laughter when he'd finally heard the tale of her scrambling to get that apartment. He must have driven her crazy.

E.J. had brought the news that all hell had broken loose at Davis, Hansen and Davis. The partners had come down hard on Robert. Drew had been fired. The firm had appealed to the bar and had had the complaint rescinded. Jared had helped matters by getting his former client a very nice settlement with her ex. He'd even been offered his job back. He'd said no. Other firms had made offers—nice ones—but he was now mulling over the possibility of opening his own offices. E.J. had already told him she would come with him. He wanted Alison for his very personal secretary. She, however, wanted to go back to school—in music.

That had come as a surprise. But then, why not? he thought. Everything about her was a surprise.

They accepted their guests' congratulations and best wishes. He was pleased his entire family had turned out. Peter and Mary Ellen stood arm in arm. Michael, Janice and all the kids were next to them, smiling and chattering. Even his parents had come, although they weren't speaking to each other. Jared grinned and kissed them both anyway. He looked around for his cousin Raymond, but Raymond wasn't in the room....

Raymond Holiday stepped out into the bright November sunshine. He remembered two other weddings, and cousins discussing the merits of bachelorhood. No one joined him today. The cold wind whipped through his suit jacket, but he liked the sharp needles riffling along his skin. They reminded him to hold to his original theories about women. His cousins might have lost their minds. But not him.

Never him. He wanted and needed no woman in his life.

Late that night, Jared dragged out his list of ideal attributes in a mate. Alison was asleep in his bed, the first of the rest of their nights together. But something had nagged him and he had come into his office. The list had caught his eye.

He glanced through the various things he'd once thought were important to his life and shook his head at the nonsense. Nothing mattered except finding the person who felt right. Alison felt very right. He tossed the list in the trash. He would have a lifetime to get to know Alison Palmer Holiday, starting with their living on the edge of financial disaster, as they were now. And to think he had been a man with a long-term, master plan.

It would be fun, he thought, while heading back to bed. To his wife, who had all the ideal attributes he could ever want in a woman.

The Justice statuette stood proudly on the desktop, not at all minding the slight interruption. It was about time Jared and Alison realized what really counted in life. People had long forgotten that her original name in ancient Greek was *Dice*. Life was truly a gamble.

She knew the last Holiday had to be brought into the

fold, but her own job was finished. She was a working girl, after all. A great job she'd done, too, if she said so herself. And she did, allowing she was hardly impartial on the subject. In fact, she was so pleased with her efforts, she decided to heck with impartiality.

She lifted her blindfold and peeked.

COMING NEXT MONTH

#697 SPUR-OF-THE-MOMENT MARRIAGE by Cathy Gillen Thacker
Wild West Weddings

Cowboy counselor Cisco Kidd never expected to be a fifteen-minute fiancé in a client's matchmaking plans. His intended, Gillian Taylor, was certainly anxious to say "I do." While her sexy sass turned on his every desire, her eyes held secrets—secrets he'd spend their required honeymoon seducing from her.

#698 PLEASE SAY "I DO" by Karen Toller Whittenburg
Three Weddings & a Hurricane

Rik Austin wouldn't let wedding planner Hallie Bernhardt disrupt his plans to disrupt this wedding. He knew just what to do—a little tequila here, a little seduction there. Before she knew it, Hallie would be bewitched and bewildered—and the wedding would be history. But a funny thing happened on the way to disaster....

#699 VERDICT: PARENTHOOD by Jule McBride
Big Apple Babies

Overnight, the "Sexiest Man in Manhattan," Grantham Hale, became the adoptive daddy of quadruplets *and* twins! But his real troubles start when the quads' presumed-dead—but very much alive—biological mother reappears and the judge sentences Phoebe and Grantham to be parents... together!

#700 MR. WRONG! by Mary Anne Wilson

Guardian angel Angelina had worked hard to turn Melanie Clark into the proper mate for "Mr. Perfect." But *now* Angelina finds out Melanie is destined for Mr. Perfect's rougher, tougher, untamed brother...a guy Melanie can recognize at forty paces as Mr. Wrong!

AVAILABLE THIS MONTH:

Look us up on-line at: http://www.romance.net

Take 4 bestselling love stories FREE

Plus get a FREE surprise gift!

Special Limited-time Offer

Mail to Harlequin Reader Service®

3010 Walden Avenue
P.O. Box 1867
Buffalo, N.Y. 14240-1867

YES! Please send me 4 free Harlequin American Romance® novels and my free surprise gift. Then send me 4 brand-new novels every month, which I will receive months before they appear in bookstores. Bill me at the low price of $3.12 each plus 25¢ delivery and applicable sales tax, if any.* That's the complete price and a savings of over 10% off the cover prices—quite a bargain! I understand that accepting the books and gift places me under no obligation ever to buy any books. I can always return a shipment and cancel at any time. Even if I never buy another book from Harlequin, the 4 free books and the surprise gift are mine to keep forever.

154 BPA A3UM

Name	(PLEASE PRINT)	
Address	Apt. No.	
City	State	Zip

This offer is limited to one order per household and not valid to present Harlequin American Romance® subscribers. *Terms and prices are subject to change without notice. Sales tax applicable in N.Y.

UAM-696

©1990 Harlequin Enterprises Limited

HARLEQUIN WOMEN KNOW ROMANCE WHEN THEY SEE IT.

And they'll see it on **ROMANCE CLASSICS**, the new 24-hour TV channel devoted to romantic movies and original programs like the special **Romantically Speaking-Harlequin® Goes Prime Time**.

Romantically Speaking-Harlequin® Goes Prime Time introduces you to many of your favorite romance authors in a program developed exclusively for Harlequin® readers.

Watch for **Romantically Speaking-Harlequin® Goes Prime Time** beginning in the summer of 1997.

If you're not receiving ROMANCE CLASSICS, call your local cable operator or satellite provider and ask for it today!

Escape to the network of your dreams.

Free Gift Offer

With a Free Gift proof-of-purchase
from any Harlequin® book, you can receive
a beautiful cubic zirconia pendant.

This stunning marquise-shaped stone is a genuine cubic
zirconia—accented by an 18" gold tone necklace.
(Approximate retail value $19.95)

Send for yours today...
compliments of ⬧HARLEQUIN®

To receive your free gift, a cubic zirconia pendant, send us one original proof-of-
purchase, photocopies not accepted, from the back of any Harlequin Romance®,
Harlequin Presents®, Harlequin Temptation®, Harlequin Superromance®, Harlequin
Intrigue®, Harlequin American Romance®, or Harlequin Historicals® title available at
your favorite retail outlet, together with the Free Gift Certificate, plus a check or money
order for $1.65 U.S./$2.15 CAN. (do not send cash) to cover postage and handling,
payable to Harlequin Free Gift Offer. We will send you the specified gift. Allow 6 to 8
weeks for delivery. Offer good until December 31, 1997, or while quantities last. Offer
valid in the U.S. and Canada only.

Free Gift Certificate

Name: _____

Address: _____

City: _____ State/Province: _____ Zip/Postal Code: _____

Mail this certificate, one proof-of-purchase and a check or money order for postage
and handling to: HARLEQUIN FREE GIFT OFFER 1997. In the U.S.: 3010 Walden
Avenue, P.O. Box 9071, Buffalo NY 14269-9057. In Canada: P.O. Box 604, Fort Erie,
Ontario L2Z 5X3.

FREE GIFT OFFER   084-KEZ

ONE PROOF-OF-PURCHASE
To collect your fabulous FREE GIFT, a cubic zirconia pendant, you must include this
original proof-of-purchase for each gift with the properly completed Free Gift Certificate.

084-KEZR

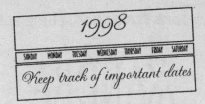

1998

SUNDAY MONDAY TUESDAY WEDNESDAY THURSDAY FRIDAY SATURDAY

Keep track of important dates

Three beautiful and colorful calendars that celebrate some of the most popular trends in America today.

Look for:

Just Babies—a 16 month calendar that features a full year of absolutely adorable babies!

1998 CALENDAR
Just Babies
16 months of adorable bundles of joy!

Hometown Quilts
1998 Calendar
A 16 month quilting extravaganza!

Hometown Quilts—a 16 month calendar featuring quilted art squares, plus a short history on twelve different quilt patterns.

Inspirations—a 16 month calendar with inspiring pictures and quotations.

Inspirations
A 16 month calendar that will lift your spirits and gladden your heart

Steeple Hill™

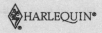 HARLEQUIN®

Value priced at $9.99 U.S./$11.99 CAN., these calendars make a perfect gift!

Available in retail outlets in August 1997.　　CAL98

New York Times bestselling author

brings a love story that will take you...

ABOVE AND BEYOND

(previously published under the pseudonym Erin St. Claire)

Letters of love—to another man—brought them together. A powerful secret may tear them apart.

Trevor Rule fell in love with Kyla before he met her, just by reading the letters she'd written to her husband—Trevor's best friend. Now he had to convince Kyla that they both had the right to be happy and move past the tragedy of Trevor's death....

**Available in September 1997
at your favorite retail outlet.**

MIRA The Brightest Stars in Women's Fiction.™